"YOU GAVE ME QUITE A TURN, MISS" said the old servant. "You look so much like her."

Emily spun around to look at her reflection in the lovely old silver-framed mirror over the dressing table. She pushed up her tumbling hair.

"Am I really so much like her?"

"I'll have to warn the mistress," said the old woman as she left.

There was something very disturbing to Emily about this enigmatic and secretive old woman.

She turned again to the mirror. "You," she said. "You aren't a ghost and had better not find yourself being treated as one. No dead woman's shoes for you, my girl. A new life for you in this glorious sunshine. Love, living, fun, freedom . . . All the things poor unlucky Dolly lost so soon."

It was a half hour later, just before she was ready to go downstairs, that the child began screaming . . .

MARY PARADISE

The
Marriage
Chest

A FAWCETT CREST BOOK
Fawcett Publications, Inc., Greenwich, Conn.
Member of American Book Publishers Council, Inc.

THIS BOOK CONTAINS THE COMPLETE TEXT OF
THE ORIGINAL HARDCOVER EDITION.

All of the characters in this book are fictitious, and any
resemblance to actual persons, living or dead,
is purely coincidental.

A Fawcett Crest Book reprinted by arrangement with
Coward-McCann, Inc.

Library of Congress Catalog Card Number: 66-20159

PRINTING HISTORY
Coward-McCann edition published August 3, 1966
First printing, August 1966
Second printing, November 1966

First Fawcett Crest Printing, February 1968

Published by Fawcett World Library
67 West 44th Street, New York, N. Y. 10036
PRINTED IN THE UNITED STATES OF AMERICA

The
Marriage
Chest

CHAPTER ONE

"GRANADA," said the guide, "is famous for many things, its cathedral where the bodies of the great Catholic sovereigns, Isabel la Catolica and Felipe, lie, the world-renowned Alhambra, the Generalife Gardens where nightingales sing . . ."

For the last twenty miles Emily had heard scarcely a word he said. She had been travelling along this long curving road that went up hillsides where stark white villages perched among nothing but bare rocks, and down again among the olive groves and orange trees, with Dolly for company. The legendary Dolly who had come to Spain fifty years ago with twenty bags and boxes, a canary in a cage, and a maid no older than herself to visit the Spanish aunt who lived in a villa called the *Casa de Flor* in Granada. If Dolly had driven down this road, it must have been a long and exhausting journey with frequent stops at the rather dubious inns they had passed. No wonder she had got typhus. Although that must have been quite a long time later, because by then she had certainly reached Granada, the elderly aunt had died and left her the *Casa de Flor,* she had fallen in love, and Cousin Hannah had hastened hotfoot to save her from a disastrous marriage.

When two weeks ago, in London, the letter had arrived from Hannah inviting her to Spain, Emily's father's immediate expostulation had been, "Stay away from the old bitch!"

Emily had heard vaguely the story of her Aunt Dolly and her trip to Spain to visit the elderly aunt who had almost immediately died and her parents' consternation when she refused to come home but announced instead her in-

7

tention of marrying some Spaniard, a flamenco dancer or a peon or just an adventurer with his eyes on Dolly's money. She had also heard of her plain cousin Hannah being dispatched to bring her back and in the end none of them returning, Hannah, Dolly, or Dolly's maid.

She hadn't realised what a fascinating story it was until the letter came from Hannah. She demanded to hear the story all over again, and her father was nothing loath to tell it.

"Hannah was no doubt tired of being a poor relation. I don't blame her. Dolly and I used to call her Hannah the Governess. But she was fond of Dolly—or professed to be. She was very willing to desert her pupils and take her little ruler to Spain and rap poor Dolly sharply on the knuckles and tell her to behave herself. Anyway, she quickly dispatched the impertinent lover, locked Dolly in her room, and starved her to death."

"Daddy, she *didn't!*"

Her father rolled his eyes, the Bowman blue eyes, a little faded now, as Dolly's would have been, too, but still ravishing.

"A moot point, my dear. A very moot point. I can well remember how Hannah looked before she set out on her travels. Dolly was the complete female, bonnets galore, veils, ruffles, kid gloves, parasols. But Hannah—straight as a board, dressed in black bombasine. Or brown, perhaps. Something funereal that wouldn't attract roving Spanish eyes."

Emily was convulsed with laughter.

"Daddy, you're exaggerating."

"Not a bit of it. That's exactly how I remember her."

"And she really did dispatch Dolly's Spaniard?"

"That's what some say. Others say she married him herself."

"The very same man! But she couldn't have! I mean, Dolly with her ruffles and Hannah the way you describe her."

"Well, something mighty odd happened. Within six months of arriving in Spain Hannah was married to a gentleman called Ferdinand Romero and Dolly had died of a broken heart."

"Surely it was typhus!"

"Hannah had to call it something, but I have my own theory. She must have been pretty jealous of Dolly. Think of it for yourself. Dolly was pretty, Hannah plain, Dolly rich, Hannah poor, Dolly had a string of admirers, and Hannah, it's pretty safe to assume, had none."

"Then that makes it all the more unlikely that she could steal Dolly's lover."

"Yes, you have a point there. My mother and father were certain he had had to be bought off with Dolly's money. She had come into her share of a legacy from our grandfather when she was twenty-one and on top of that old Aunt Isabella left her the villa in Granada. So she was quite a catch for an enterprising Spaniard. But in the end no one got her. What happened before her death, no one knows, except Hannah. But Dolly left Hannah the villa, either in gratitude, or to keep her mouth shut. I don't know which. So she was able to live in luxurious surroundings for the first time in her unselfish life."

"She and her husband, this Ferdinand?"

"That's right."

"But didn't anyone go out and see for themselves what had really happened?"

"I would have if I'd been old enough. I was a boy of twelve at school. My father, who was impossibly Puritan, privately thought Dolly had got the end she deserved. My mother had always been uncomfortable about having such a beautiful daughter so unlike herself. She was timid and completely dominated by my father. Old Barrett of Wimpole Street had nothing on Papa. Dolly was a meteor flashing through their lives and they never knew it."

"And through Hannah's, too, I imagine," Emily observed. "Hannah should have been their daughter."

"I should have gone out when I was older," her father said reflectively. "But somehow I could never bring myself to be civil to Hannah. I'd probably have ended by accusing her of murdering Dolly."

"Daddy! No!"

"Well, maybe it wouldn't have been true. But Dolly shouldn't have died at twenty-two. Scratching up that red Spanish dirt to bury her at twenty-two!" Emily's father's face was dark with the helplessness of an old anger. "While wily Hannah thrived and prospered."

"But that was to her credit. She had a business brain."

"Yes. I grant her that. She started an antique business and made it pay. I've seen her name in sales at Sotheby's from time to time. She must be pretty old now, but she has a son and a son-in-law to carry on."

"She sounds a fascinating old woman," Emily said.

"I've no doubt she is. But why the devil should she be suddenly interested in you?"

"She read about my accident in the paper. I think she's sorry for me."

Her father reared up indignantly.

"Good God, how dare she be sorry for a girl like you! Look what you've got; a perfect body, good height, long legs, plenty of poise, a sense of humour, intelligence, the Bowman eyes. What else could anyone want? No, baby, I haven't forgotten your finger. But the injury doesn't show, and all it means is that you won't have to sit at a piano for the rest of your life. Which I must admit I never thought was any life for an attractive woman."

Emily leaned forward to kiss her father. She knew that the sudden end to her career had upset him almost as much as it had herself. But he would despise self-pity. And so would she.

"Anyway, she says I remind her of Dolly. I suppose she's getting sentimental in her old age. I think I'd like to go, Daddy."

"She's offering you a job teaching her grandchild. She's turning the tables, making you, Dolly's niece, into the governess."

"No, I don't think so. I think she's making it easy for me to accept her hospitality."

"You're kind, Emily. You're still young enough to be kind. I'm an old cynic, I suppose. But, I warn you, don't be too innocent where Hannah is concerned. Get as much as you can out of her. She owes it to us, or I'm a Dutchman."

So that was why, as the light died over the Sierras, and the bus entered the outskirts of the city, Dolly's story was more in Emily's mind than thoughts of the Moorish victory over Andalusia.

She began to take an active interest in her surroundings then, and saw the strings of over-laden donkeys meekly plodding home behind their masters in the dusk, the small white-washed cottages with doorways open into ink-black interiors, the brown-faced, black-eyed children playing in the dust, the bursts of brilliant flowers cascading over tumble-down buildings.

The road widened and became busier as they approached the centre of the city. Since she had preferred to make the overland journey instead of travelling by air, Hannah had written that Fabrice would meet her in the square where the bus stopped.

Emily had understood that Fabrice, his mother's first child, was approaching fifty. The man who stood a little apart, proclaiming his Englishness by his hair bleached to a straw colour, his deeply tanned skin and blue eyes, was much younger than that. Perhaps he wasn't waiting for her at all.

But there was no one else who hadn't already vociferously claimed some passenger. Emily and the stranger were left staring at one another.

He was the first to speak.

"I think you must be Miss Bowman."

She nodded.

"I'm Patrick Fermoyle. Lucie's husband." He held out his hand, but didn't smile. He was assessing her quite frankly, but his eyes remained curiously cool, almost unfriendly.

"Is that all your luggage?" He indicated the two bags at her feet.

"Yes. I thought Fabrice was coming to meet me."

"He had an unexpected appointment. But you'll be seeing him at dinner. Let's go, shall we?"

There was still no smile, just that cool politeness, and a vertical line between his eyes. Patrick Fermoyle, her cousin Lucie's husband, didn't welcome her particularly. She wondered why.

He was carrying the bags across to the car.

"Have a good journey?" he asked perfunctorily.

"Yes, wonderful. I loved every minute of it. It's my first visit to Spain." His very unfriendliness made her go on vivaciously, "I'm terribly grateful to Cousin Hannah for making it possible. I admit I was in rather a low state about this wretched finger." She held out her hand. "It's such a silly little—" She realized he wasn't listening. He had put her bags in the back of the car and was holding the door open for her. She got in silently and he went round to get in the other side.

"You were saying you had hurt your finger?"

"Nothing to speak of." She could be aloof, too. She wasn't begging him to sympathise with her. "Is it your daughter who is to have the music lessons?"

"Juana. That seems to be the general idea."

"But not your idea?"

He looked at her then.

"How did you work that out?"

"I just got an impression."

"Clever. As it happens, you're right. My daughter, as you will find out soon enough, is a very spoilt little girl. She needs to be sent to a good strict boarding school. I'm sorry if I seem to harp on this subject over the next few weeks. It's a thing I feel rather strongly about. Does that make me an unnatural father?" His blue eyes were not indifferent now. They stared at her demandingly.

"It's hardly a reason for you to be so unfriendly to me," Emily murmured.

He pressed the starting button with an impatient gesture.

"What shall I say? Welcome to Granada? Welcome to the gypsies and the nightingales and the nights scented with jasmine and orange blossom?"

She was astonished by his vehemence. She thought him rude, bad-tempered, a boor. Yet she was suddenly much too conscious of him beside her. In spite of his tan and look of health his face was very thin. A pulse throbbed low down in one cheek. His hands on the steering wheel were tense. There was a streak of yellow paint on one thumb. He was dressed for the heat in an open-necked shirt and obviously very old slacks. He should have looked relaxed and easy. Instead, he was knotted up over something; the heat perhaps, or having to meet her when he disapproved of her coming, or his problem daughter, or Hannah's or his wife's highhandedness about the music lessons. She found herself wishing very much that she knew what it was.

"It's only you who doesn't want me here, I hope," she said tentatively.

"Miss Bowman, let's get this straight. As for wanting you, I can only speak for myself, and that's simply because of the ethics of the thing. I might as well tell you about it now. You'll find it out for yourself soon enough." He felt in his pocket for cigarettes. "Smoke?"

"No, thank you."

He took out a cigarette and lit it before he went on.

"My mother-in-law has thought up this brilliant idea herself. She's a very organising person and prefers presenting people with a *fait accompli*. I've spent months persuading Lucie that Juana must be sent away for her own good. She has screaming fits at the slightest provocation, and hysterics or worse if her mother's out of her sight for more than half an hour at a time. She's delicate, I admit, and she always will be unless she can grow out of this obsession for her mother. But instead of listening to me, Lucie has listened to Hannah, and thinks that putting Juana's musical education in hand is going to be the solution to the whole thing."

"And it isn't?" Emily said.

"What have I just been telling you? The child's encouraged to let her emotions eat her up. That's literally what they're doing. She looks like a consumptive waif."

"Why does she have such intense emotions? She must be unhappy, or insecure, or something."

"That sounds like jargon. You're not a child psychologist, are you, as well as a piano teacher?"

Emily had been making herself keep calm during his outburst. Who was the one with emotions, she had been thinking, he or his daughter? But now suddenly his weary sarcastic voice made her own none too reliable temper flare.

"Don't upset yourself, Mr Fermoyle. I'm not a child psychologist. I'm not even a piano teacher. You see, I foolishly let a taxi fall on my middle finger. It's quite a tragedy when you come to think of it. I was booked for a season of concerts in London and later Salzburg and Vienna. But the taxi tipped over, and that was that. I was really very lucky that of all the people involved in the accident none of us had more than bruises, and my crushed finger. The point of all this is that I don't particularly look forward to teaching what sounds like a horrible child her five-finger exercises. It's quite a come-down for me. But I did seize the very welcome chance Cousin Hannah gave me to run away from London. It had got a little painful to me temporarily. All my friends were in orchestras or involved with music in some way. So I was glad to escape." But, she turned sharply on him, "I simply won't sit here and be blamed for coming and upsetting your own plans. It sounds as if you and your wife have simply made a mess of bringing up your child and that's absolutely nothing to do with me. So now—perhaps we can go, and I can meet Cousin Hannah."

Although the engine was running he made no attempt to put the car into gear.

"You were showing me your finger before."

"You must excuse me. It's a nervous habit I'll get over."

"I'm sorry about it. No one told me."

"Perhaps you simply didn't listen."

"Perhaps. That's quite likely. I've got a filthy temper. I've been working like a galley slave on this exhibition—oh, the hell with it! But if you think things will be easy in Cousin Hannah's romantic villa, the *Casa de Flor,* you're wrong."

It was the nearest he could come to making an apology, she recognized. He had an awkward stubborn pride. Apologies were anathema to her, too, but since he had made a gesture she also would have to.

"I don't want things easy, Patrick. I just want them interesting."

"Oh, they'll be that. I can promise you that."

He didn't reciprocate with the gift of her name, but he did give her a long measuring look before he at last started the car. She wished suddenly that she didn't look so travel-stained.

CHAPTER TWO

Two hours before Emily's arrival Hannah lay in bed making the momentous decision to get up and dress for dinner.

She would wear a long dress, the Chanel, she thought, her jade ear-rings and grey lace mantilla. She would carry a fan, the one from the Duchess of Alba's collection. Fabrice was angry when she used it, knowing its value. But she had always said she would enjoy, as well as make money from, the beautiful things she handled.

Anyway, manipulating a fan was good for her weak hand, the doctor said. Better than using that ugly lump of putty. She wouldn't have Emily arrive and find her squeezing putty in her fingers like a child.

Nor would she have Emily meet her for the first time in bed. She would be sitting in her chair giving audience, as Lucie described it. She wanted Emily to be impressed.

No one was quite sure nowadays how much Hannah heard and saw. She enjoyed fooling the doctor, and Patterson, too. Her hearing and eyesight were as good as they had ever been. Looking out of her window she could see the lovely line of the Sierras as clearly as she had seen them the day she arrived in Granada. She could see the faded amber and dust-coloured roofs, the acacia trees, a string of donkeys in the square, the church towers (there was always a church, no matter how poor the Spanish village, the houses huddled round it like people round a fire). She could hear the sound of bells, and Maria chattering ceaselessly in the garden, and cars accelerating their engines to get up the steep hill to the Alhambra Palace and the Generalife Gardens. Tourists. She wasn't interested in tourists. Her prices were too high for them. They wanted to discover some cute antique for a few pesetas, a relic of Moorish Spain for a dime. She wouldn't have tourists mentioned.

Patterson fought with Hannah daily to close the shutters during siesta. But she preferred the view to keeping cool. That glorious sun-drenched country stretched from here to the high Sierras. She could see the road the funeral procession had taken when Isabella of Spain's body had been brought for burial in the vaults of Granada Cathedral, a body humbly clad in a nun's habit. (Would she have a similar humility? Hannah wondered, and doubted it.) She could see the plains the Moors had swept over to conquer Andalusia and leave their indelible stamp on the province in their incomparable palaces and gardens, their gentle fountains, their still pools of water that were mirrors more beautiful and subtle than anything designed by Chippendale. She could see the cypresses, dark unlit candles that were the guardians of every church in Spain, the orange trees, the eucalypti, the fiery bursts of bougainvillaea, and the blue-purple of the morning glory. She could see and smell the heat.

And Patterson told her to keep the shutters closed!

Apart from sight, she could hear everything that went on in the house. Or almost everything. What she didn't hear she guessed. Or Patterson told her. Patterson, her protagonist in a thousand arguments, her constant guardian, her apparently willing slave. Though who knew after all these years who was mistress and who servant? Hannah believed Patterson was genuinely grieved when Hannah had what the doctor carefully called her small cerebral accident. But she would be, of course. They had been together for fifty years. They were tied by countless things. It would scarcely please Patterson for Hannah to die. So, brought back to life and almost suffocated by Patterson's vigilance which she could not do without, Hannah shrugged her tired shoulders and said they lived to fight another day.

Anyway, Patterson was nearly as old as Hannah. What right had she to assume that her mistress would go first? She was getting breathless, with all that superfluous flesh she carried. She tried to hide this fact, but Hannah noticed. Hannah was observant, too.

"If you want to outlive me, Patterson," she told her, "you'll have to eat less *paella,* less *churros* for breakfast."

But then Patterson would start on her endless lament for English food. As if she had been forcibly kept in Spain. As if she couldn't have gone home after Dolly had died. Hannah wasn't used to being pampered with the services of a maid, as Dolly had been. But Patterson had begged to stay. She said that, like Hannah, she had nothing to go home for. She had promised to make herself useful to Hannah. And she had. There was no question of that.

Hannah could hear her coming now. She pretended not to. If everyone believed that she had grown a little deaf she would overhear secrets. And she wanted to hear every one of them. It was important that she should.

"Madam!" Patterson repeated more loudly, "Madam!"

Hannah's eyes were slits. Nevertheless, she saw clearly the large form bending over her, the heavy arms in the long-sleeved grey dress, the thrusting bosom beneath the starched white apron (a bosom never fondled by a man, which perhaps explained partially Patterson's obsessive attention—attention, not devotion, Hannah thought dryly—to her mistress). She was like a solid grey shadow, always there, almost Hannah's own shadow, enormously inflated.

"You don't need to shout at me, Patterson," she said reprovingly. "I've been awake for hours."

"I'm not surprised, if you will let all the heat in."

"I am like the old Arabs, Patterson. I like to see my enemy approaching."

"Oh, aye. I've heard that before. But even taken unawares you'd still be a match for most enemies, madam."

"Only for most, Patterson? You think I can be defeated now because I have a lame leg and a hand that doesn't behave itself?"

"You have to face facts, madam. Age defeats us all."

"It won't defeat me, Patterson. Don't start getting ideas. I'm not finished yet. I have several important things to do before I go to lie beside Ferdie. And that reminds me, tomorrow is the day for the cemetery. Remember to order flowers."

"They won't last two hours in this hot sun, madam."

"I seem to have heard that remark before, Patterson. And I've told you that I refuse to buy some monstrous artificial wreath in a glass dome to lay on my darling Ferdie. What if the flowers do die!"

"You're not planning to take them yourself, madam, I hope."

"Why not? In another hour I propose to get up and bathe and dress. I shall go downstairs to dinner tonight."

"Madam!" Patterson was horrified. "The doctor—"

"The doctor encourages a little exercise in my room. What will this be but a little exercise? Bother you, woman!" Hannah struggled up, but was infuriatingly dependent on Patterson's help. All the same, she was able to say in a clear strong voice, "Am I to eat alone up here like a pariah, when Dolly's niece arrives? I shall be downstairs. And looking my best. Now"—she had to admit to a little breathlessness— "I have no objection to taking a little something to sustain me in the meantime."

Patterson's unwrinkled face, as round as an apple, its skin retaining its fresh red in spite of the remorseless heat, was trained to be expressionless. But Hannah knew very well, from fifty years' study, the expressions that were suppressed. A slight tightening of the good-natured mouth, a stare from the pebble-grey eyes, the faintest sniff—she had long ago got Patterson out of her tendency to sniff by telling her it was a spinsterish habit, but under stress the habit persisted. These signs represented disapproval, or stubbornness, or just plain shock. Hannah reflected with satisfaction that she could still shock someone who had been her intimate companion for so long.

"Very well, madam," Patterson said now, preparing to leave the room. "I will help you to dress if you insist. But I'll be taking flowers for two to the cemetery before I know it."

Hannah lifted her head on its thin old neck, as browned and folded with age as a lizard's throat, and gave her cackle of laughter.

"Remember I can't endure lilies," she shouted after Patterson.

But it was aggravating how tired she got. Perhaps it was the heat. The silk sheets felt damp beneath her and the pillow in its hand-embroidered silk case uncomfortably hot. She pushed aside the coverlet, although it was only lace, cobwebby and yellowed, older than she could remember, and very expensive. She had acquired some nice things in her half century of business. It pleased her vanity, for instance, to sleep in this bed. It was eighteenth-century Venetian with a carved gilt and damask headboard. Of the same period was an Italian painted commode, and a wardrobe decorated with garlands of roses. Fabrice's favourite clock stood on the commode. He had hated giving it to her; he was no businessman, he could scarcely bear to part with any of his clocks, even at a handsome profit. But this one was an artistic gem, a Louis the Fifteenth porcelain-mounted lion clock. The bronze lion stood on an elaborate base, and the white porcelain roses curved round the clock's face. There was also a French Empire couch covered in red silk, old silky Kirman rugs on the well-polished floor, a silver-framed Florentine mirror over the dressing table, heavy damask drapes at the long windows. The chandelier, like the bed, was eighteenth-century Venetian.

It was a beautiful room. It represented a life's work.

It was a pity she and Ferdie couldn't have slept in a room like this the night of their marriage. . . .

The voices were in her head again. She stirred, and threshed her arms, but she couldn't shut them out. They had been becoming more and more insistent lately. Sometimes she had a moment of terrifying confusion, not knowing which was the past and which the present.

"So you're really going to marry him, Hannah. You meant it all the time."

Dolly's voice wasn't so much resentful as perplexed. She had obviously never expected anyone to marry Hannah. She could have a dozen proposals and refuse them all. She hadn't thought of Hannah having the opportunity to refuse even one.

Hannah whipped up her resentful thoughts so that she wouldn't be snared by pity for Dolly's white face and drowned blue eyes.

"Of course I'm going to marry him. I don't play fast and loose with men."

"The way I do, you're suggesting." Dolly's voice was unbearably humble. "Yes, I know I have at times, but I didn't with Jaime. I promise I didn't. He just—disappeared."

"And good riddance," Hannah said roughly.

"I expect you're right. You usually are. Don't scold me, Hannah. I really do try to keep away from the window. I've told Patterson to only open the shutters after dark. I don't know which is the worst, sitting in this gloom listening, or staring out until the sunlight seems to burn up my eyes."

"I told you he won't come back," Hannah said, turning away abruptly from Dolly's bowed head. *"How could you think he would? Spanish grandees expect their women to be unsullied."*

"Unsullied!" The word tripped on Dolly's tongue. *"What an absurd word. Only you would use it. And it was only once —without Patterson. Only once I met him. He—promised—"*

"Then don't make remarks about my Ferdie. He keeps his promises."

"Yes, I know. I do know, Hannah dear. I'm sure he's good and kind. I hope you'll be awfully happy. I want to give you a beautiful wedding present. What would you like?"

"Nothing!" Hannah said violently.

"Oh, Hannah darling! You do have a soft heart after all. You're almost crying. Let me give you something awfully pretty to be married in."

"Ferdie hasn't the money to spend on a new suit. He won't want a fashionable bride. I'll wear my Sunday dress. That will do very well."

"Then a nightgown. One of my own special nightgowns. I had them embroidered in Majorca. Have one of them, Hannah," Dolly pleaded. *"You can't be a bride without a new nightgown. And that old marriage chest I found. You can make more use of it than I can. . . ."*

Hannah moved sharply, willing the voices in her head to be silent. This was no time to be going over old grudges and grievances, when Emily was arriving and something new was beginning.

Yes, something new and fresh in her tired life.

All the same, she had to go on remembering her wedding night, how Ferdie had comforted her about the bare floor of their bedroom, the austere furniture, the airless heat, and the apparent sleeplessness of Spaniards who sat up until after midnight in the courtyard beneath their window talking vociferously.

"The other things will come, my darling. With patience."

Ferdie had grown very proud of his good English. He preferred to use English endearments, too, which he spoke with a parrot-like lack of expression. He would be much more passionate in his own language, she was sure, but as she didn't yet understand Spanish he courteously used English. In the meantime she must be thankful that they could communicate at all.

All the same, it wasn't entirely easy being contented with the horrid little room when she thought of Dolly in her luxurious villa inherited from Aunt Isabella. As if she hadn't enough already. All the same, Hannah was glad she had had sufficient pride to refuse a wedding present.

But she did wear Dolly's nightgown, and refused to let Ferdie remove it. What did he think she was, a whore?

She got over those delicate feelings soon enough. She learned to speak Spanish and found that Ferdie was indeed much more passionate in his own language. With the hot sun and Ferdie's tuition her inhibitions fell away. She had never been good-looking, but Ferdie taught her how to make her plainness an asset. The older she grew the plainer she grew, and this delighted him. He said she was so divinely ugly she was beautiful. He exaggerated, of course. He always had, and perhaps most of all, she realised many years later, on their wedding night. But that no longer mattered because by the time he died their strange awkward marriage had been a success.

So he deserved the tribute of fresh flowers, once a week, on his grave.

Patterson was returning, carrying a tray. She set it down beside the bed and Hannah looked with approval at its contents: the George the Third silver teapot and milk jug (she had brought that back from one of her forays in London), the egg-shell china, the thin slices of lemon, the cucumber sandwiches. An English tea in the heart of Spain. It pleased her.

"What is everybody doing? I can't hear a thing up here."

"The usual, madam. Mr Fabrice is at the shop, and Mr Patrick painting. Miss Lucie said something about going shopping when it got a bit cooler, that was if the child was better. She had one of her turns at lunchtime."

"A convulsion?"

"Whatever you call it, madam. She lay on the floor kicking and had to be carried to her room. Miss Lucie's been with her ever since."

"And what was the cause this time?" Hannah asked wearily.

"Something her father said about sending her to school.

He said it was nonsense this young woman coming out to teach her the piano, she should be packed off to boarding school and taught a great many other things, including manners."

"An intelligent observation. I entirely agree. But you know Lucie won't part with her."

"She keeps her a baby, Madam. She's nearly eight, after all."

"Yes, yes, yes. We've said that many times. I know what I would do if the child were mine. But since she's not and her mother's determined to spoil her, we can only do what we can to arrest the process. If she is considered too delicate to go to school, then she must have some sort of education at home. I hope Emily Bowman is partly the answer, though if she's too much like her Aunt Dolly she may be another complication. We must just wait and see."

"Yes, madam. Aren't you going to drink your tea?"

"In a moment. You don't approve of Emily coming, do you, Patterson?"

"It's nothing to do with me, madam."

"Don't be a hypocrite, Patterson. You make my business very much your business. Out with it. Tell me what you're thinking. You will eventually. We might as well get it over now."

Patterson drew herself up, her fine bosom thrust out beneath her white apron, her face solemnly righteous.

"It doesn't seem right, madam, that Miss Dolly's niece should come here as a servant."

Hannah's dark face contorted. Almost at once she overcame the spasm of anger. Anger was dangerous for her now. And what Patterson had said was perfectly true, within limits. Patterson, the old fool, was still dazzled by Dolly's charm. It was a pity Dolly hadn't lived to grow old. One would have seen then whose personality was the most effective: Dolly, faded and sweet, or Hannah, with her triumphant dominant ugliness.

She spoke incredulously. "Are you suggesting I'm having some sort of petty revenge because of the way Dolly and her family treated me? Hannah the poor relation, Hannah the governess. But that's centuries ago, and has nothing to do with this child. If you must know, I admired Dolly enormously. I longed to be like her, with her pink and white skin and fair hair and those great blue eyes. And her waist. She used to let her young men measure it in their hands.

Everyone thought she was so bold, but I knew she was just naïve and silly. After all, I was qualified to sum up a person's mental ability. I had had enough experience."

Patterson's lowered eyelids hid the expression in her eyes. Hannah had a certain feeling that it was insolent. But Patterson was much too clever to allow such an expression to show. She said in her passionless voice:

"You're talking too much, madam. You should be resting before you dress. If you still intend to dress."

"Of course I intend to dress," Hannah said irritably. "And if I don't talk I'll think, which is just as bad. Get me that newspaper cutting, and Dolly's photograph."

When Patterson had brought them she lay looking at them for a long time. Dolly's picture was faded. It had been taken when she was dressed for a garden party. She wore a huge floppy hat and carried a parasol. Her face, shadowed by the hat, was round with youth and laughing. Hannah's memory filled in the details of the perfect skin, the rosy lips, the gorgeous blue eyes that turned violet when Dolly wore her favourite lavender colours.

The newspaper picture of the girl at the piano was different and yet not different. She was dressed with severity in a sweater and skirt. None of Dolly's beloved frills and flounces there. She was serious, too. The cutting said that she had had a promising career ahead of her as a pianist, so naturally her face had a dedicated look. For all that, the sweet youthful oval of it, the dreaming eyes, and the crown of thick blonde hair were shatteringly Dolly's. It was as if time had turned back.

And to Hannah's intense surprise, she found that she passionately wanted time to turn back. No, she wasn't, as Patterson suggested, having an old worn-out revenge on Dolly by inviting her niece to come in a menial capacity. She was feeling her way towards rehabilitating the girl who, the newspaper said, had suffered a tragic accident to one of her hands. The nerve in the middle finger had been permanently injured. She would never play on a concert platform again.

Immediately she had seen the paper Hannah had sat down and written the letter. She had had to explain who she was since she doubted if the family ever mentioned her. There had been that terrible coldness after Dolly's death, especially when it was revealed that Dolly had left her the villa in Granada. Of course she had known that their antagonism sprang from their guilt at feeling a little relieved that they were done forever with Dolly's scandals. They really were the most revolting puritans; Uncle Edwin with his political ambitions and Aunt Kate his obedient shadow. Eugene, Dolly's brother, was only a boy at that time and probably knew very little about the affair. The ironic thing was that he, too, had had a great deal of Dolly's extravagance and wildness and she had heard that he had more or less dissipated his fortune.

So Emily, his daughter, apart from being overwhelmingly disappointed at having her career cut short, would probably be happy to earn a little for herself.

The important thing, Hannah had written firmly, was to get completely away from her surroundings. *"I came here forty-nine years ago on a visit,"* she wrote, *"and here I am still. What's more, I quickly got myself a husband, my beloved Ferdie, in spite of the fact that I was poor and plain and in England would have had little chance at all. So if your father doesn't still subscribe to the family's belief that I murdered his sister and stole her lover, then I am sure he will make no objection to your coming."*

Hannah beckoned to Patterson to come and look again at the photographs.

"The likeness grows," she said triumphantly.

Patterson nodded reluctantly.

"It will be like having a ghost around. I can't think how you want it, madam. It's morbid."

"It's a miracle, Patterson. I'm quite sure two wicked old women like us don't deserve a miracle."

"Don't make me share your sins," Patterson snapped.

Hannah lay surveying her thoughtfully. Her eyes were dulled with age and poor health, but occasionally they could shine with their old topaz brilliance. They did so now, yet her voice was creamy, bland.

"I apologise, Patterson. I exaggerated, as always. Of course I won't make you share my sins. I enjoy them too much to share them with anyone. If you're going to commit sins you must do it with panache. Make them dazzling ones, not dreary little ones." She made Patterson look at her, holding her gaze until Patterson's eyes slid away.

"The tea's cold, madam. I'll take the tray downstairs."

"Wait, Patterson. We haven't talked about your nephew today. You said you had had a letter from him. What are his new scholastic triumphs?"

"You laugh at me for doting on the boy," Patterson said sulkily.

"Far from it, Patterson. I expect to dote on Emily in exactly the same way." Her words held a challenge which Patterson chose to ignore. She merely said:

"Raymond is my only kith and kin. It's natural I should feel a responsibility for him, especially since his father went wrong. His mother is my baby sister. She was only a mite when I left home with Miss Dolly. Stands to reason I'd want to help her when her husband ran off. She wasn't so young to get a job and support a baby. I've helped Raymond through school and to get his architect's degree, so I feel he's mine in a sort of way. He's turned out well and I'm partly responsible. I'm proud of that. But you know all this, madam."

"Yes, I've heard it all before. We old people repeat ourselves. The world has changed, hasn't it? Dolly's niece has to give piano lessons and your nephew has a university education. But you haven't told me his latest news. He must have written for some reason."

"I hardly liked to bother you, madam. You were so full of Miss Emily's arrival. Raymond just said that he has made up his mind to travel this summer. He's at the stage where he needs to see different styles of architecture."

Hannah's eyes closed, hiding their momentary anger and distaste.

"Particularly Moorish?" she said dryly.

"That's right, madam. It was my idea, actually. I said if he was coming abroad he mustn't miss Spain. His old aunt would like to see him, for one thing."

"You spoil him, Patterson. Can I make a guess that this trip is being paid for out of your hard-earned savings?"

"He's a good boy," said Patterson primly. "And what else would I spend my savings on? But I didn't mean to talk about this today, madam, with you full of Miss Emily's arrival. Raymond hasn't made his plans yet."

"So he is coming here."

"Well, madam, he must see the Alhambra Palace, mustn't he? One of the wonders of the world. Though I expect he'll still go back to England and build glass boxes. But at least he'll have seen other things. Travel's broadening. We found that, didn't we?"

This time Patterson made no attempt to hide her insolent mocking expression. Anger flared uncontrollably in Hannah.

"You forget yourself, Patterson. If you're not careful, I'll dismiss you."

Patterson said nothing, merely giving her cool stare that this time did not slide away.

"Old servant or not—" Hannah screamed. But her anger had made her heart thump and she couldn't go on. She closed her eyes, shutting out Patterson's slow smile. Her thumping heart prevented her from saying that it was breathlessness, not intimidation, that had made her give way.

When Patterson had gone Hannah lay back, feeling immeasurably tired. The room seemed to have grown dark. She closed her eyes and must instantly have fallen asleep, for she was dreaming of Emily, Dolly's fair-haired niece, wandering through the Alhambra Palace hand in hand with a young man whom she knew to be Patterson's ambitious nephew. And she was trying to say, "Is this what it's all come to after fifty years of hard work?" But her tongue was too dry to move in her mouth. She was only aware of angry disapproval and again that lurking fear.

When she woke she could hear Juana screaming.

She reached over and rang the little silver bell by her bedside. She had to shake it vigorously for half a minute before Patterson came.

"Where is everyone?" she demanded irritably. "Am I to be left to die here alone?"

"Now, madam, I came as soon as I heard your bell above the child's noise."

"What's she screaming about?"

"She's getting nervous about Miss Bowman arriving. You know how she is with strangers."

"And so she screams. A child of almost eight years old. And no one can control her. What's the matter with this house?"

"You ask that, madam," Patterson said imperturbably. "Shall I run your bath?"

"Yes. And put out my clothes. The Chanel gown. I shall rest for an hour when I've dressed. When did you say the bus got in?"

"I've told you a dozen times, madam. At seven-thirty."

"Fine. That will give Emily time to change for dinner. And Fabrice is meeting her?"

"No, madam, didn't he tell you? He has a customer coming in."

Hannah made a gesture of anger.

"Patterson, no one tells me anything! They think I'm finished, lying up here. Who is this customer? Is he so important that no one else can attend to him? What is he wanting to buy? An El Greco?" The sarcasm was sharp in her voice.

"I wouldn't know, madam. But they say he's rich."

"Has he been here before? Does Fabrice know him?"

Patterson was carefully laying the Chanel gown, so deep a purple as to be almost black, across the couch.

"I should think he could tell you that himself, madam." Patterson's voice was expressionless. But Patterson knew very well, Hannah thought malevolently, that she and Fabrice had quarrelled. It had happened just before Hannah's seizure, her cerebral accident, as the doctor grandiloquently called it. Probably it was the cause of it.

Hannah had made that unfortunate mistake about the pair of Derby frilled vases. One of them had been a fake, which made the pair worth less than a quarter of what Hannah had paid for them. It was her second mistake in the last few months. She had been so sure about the small Tiepolo, too, but Patrick had proved it was not genuine.

The two misjudgments had proved expensive, and when she had needed money and taken it as usual, Fabrice had said that she would end by bankrupting them all. She, who *was* the business! Where would any of them have been without hers and Ferdie's work?

She remembered their first small shop just off the square, where they sold a few moderately-priced antiques to tourists. They had wanted the tourists then, and had done business with all the vigorous noise of the square around them, the gypsies selling castanets, the cries of the caged birds on the pavement, the men with their trays of cheap toys and novelties shrilly shouting their wares.

But Hannah was not content with mediocrity and neither was Ferdie. As soon as they had accumulated a little capital they launched into more valuable goods, pieces of seventeenth- and eighteenth-century furniture, porcelain and ceramics. They scoured the country, looking for bargains. At the beginning Ferdie had the superior knowledge, but Hannah rapidly caught up on him, and it was Hannah who had the wonderful triumph of finding the Avila Madonna. That ancient piece of carved wood, twelve inches long, brought nine thousand pounds at Sotheby's, where Ferdie had insisted it must be sold. And they were established.

It was as if that success had lit some inner eye in Hannah, and she developed a remarkable flair for discovering and buying treasures at moderate prices, and selling them not at all moderately to a carefully built-up clientele. The Bowman Galleries, as she called them, preferring her name to Ferdie's, became known internationally. When she was a rich woman she indulged herself in the furnishing of her house, poor Dolly's villa bequeathed to her long ago. Some day, she had said, she might be very glad she had assets in the form of tapestries and carpets.

There was more to it than that, of course. It stemmed from her wedding night when Hannah had worn Dolly's nightgown. She had determined then to have everything of her own, and that only of the best. There would be no more black bombasine dresses while other people wore silk. No more humiliations. Her husband would not again take her to bed in a borrowed nightgown.

So she had acquired her treasures, both as a pleasure and an investment.

It looked as if the day when she must treat them as an investment had come.

And that went back to Ferdie's death, when Fabrice had tried to take his place in the shop. But Fabrice had none of his father's drive or acumen. He was slow, quiet, heavily-built, with what Hannah despairingly called a boy's mind.

"What's the matter with your baby, Hannah? Isn't he ever going to come? He must be very large, very slow. . . .

Dolly lifted her eyelids, as if it were they and not Hannah's baby, which were so heavy. The sun had drained all the colour from her cheeks, in spite of Hannah, or Patterson, always seeing that she wore one of her large decorative hats or held her parasol in her thin slender hands.

"He'll come," Hannah said briefly.

"Yes, I suppose so. You and Ferdie must be so happy. . . ."

The baby, Fabrice, was indeed large and lethargic, right from birth. He grew up with a passion for fiddling with clocks and musical boxes. Show him any clock and he could name its maker and date. But let him try to assess the value of a sixteenth-century crucifix or a Tabriz rug, and he was hopeless.

It meant Hannah had to do all the work herself, and she was no longer young. She had counted a great deal on Patrick, her son-in-law, but he, too, had disappointed her. He preferred painting his own pictures to discovering ancient masterpieces.

And there was the way this large house ate up money. And Lucie's extravagance, and Fabrice's miserliness. And now her doctor's bills, and the endless other reasons for needing money. And that infuriating mistake about the Derby vases which had made Fabrice remind her she was an old woman with failing eyesight.

No one but herself seemed to realise the terrible seriousness of it all. The doctor had said she mustn't worry. Worry! What did he know, the bossy little fool?

So now Fabrice had thought it wise not to tell her that he had a rich customer. That she wouldn't stand. She must know what the man was looking for, and someone must find it. She and Ferdie had boasted that they could find anything from an Egyptian sarcophagus to a genuine T'ang horse. But Fabrice was different, and she was old and times had changed.

However, she could still manage Fabrice when she made the effort. And Patterson, too.

"So you know more about our customers than I do myself," she said silkily, changing the direction of her attack. "How does that happen?"

"I overheard Mr. Fabrice making the appointment on the telephone, madam. Then he called to Miss Lucie and said would she do something about that girl—about Miss Emily arriving this evening, madam, as he would be fully occupied. You'll wear your flat shoes, I hope, madam."

"With the Chanel! Don't be ridiculous. And so this obscure conversation told you that the customer was rich."

"Well, if you want to break your neck on the stairs, madam. High heels with that bad leg of yours going its own sweet way! Who is being ridiculous?"

"Patterson, answer my question."

"Oh, as to that, Miss Lucie said couldn't she or Mr. Patrick look after the customer and Mr. Fabrice said no, he was a well-known English collector, a Mr. Digby Field, and very rich."

Hannah was drumming her fingers on the bedside table. Her temples felt tight, as if she would have another seizure. When she was dead, she was dead. But she wouldn't be treated as deceased a moment before that calamitous occasion. Fabrice must come to her room at once, and keep her informed of everything that went on.

But if Digby Field were well known how was it she hadn't heard of him? Doubts niggled at her. Had she known him and forgotten? Was her memory not to be trusted?

That was nonsense. She could remember so much farther back than that—the bright day when she and Dolly had met in Madrid and Dolly had hugged her and laughed and cried, and said, "Did you come specially for my wedding, Hannah? Or to talk me out of it. Don't think you have any chance of doing that."

"Patterson, stop fiddling with my clothes and go and tell Fabrice I want to see him. And why is that water trickling away in the bathroom?"

"You asked me to run your bath, madam."

"Already! I don't want it for at least an hour. You're getting deaf, Patterson. Now hurry and send Fabrice up. And tell Lucie to make that child be quiet," she screamed after Patterson's waddling bulk.

Fabrice took his time about coming. He was still sulking, she supposed. But when he stood beside her bed, a bulky figure in his crumpled linen suit (like Patterson he was too fond of *paellas* and oily foods), his expression was its habitual pleasant, slightly melancholy one.

"Well, Mama, how are you feeling tonight?"

"I'm feeling fine. I'm coming down to dinner." Before Fabrice could express surprise about that, she went straight to the point. "Who is this Digby Field? Why haven't I been told about him?"

"Because I only heard from him this afternoon. But don't get excited. He's only interested in clocks." His gaze rested on the beautiful rose-wreathed one on the commode. "I'd like to show him that one, if you've no objection."

"It isn't for sale—not yet, anyway."

"If you keep on taking so much money out of the business it will have to be," Fabrice said flatly.

"I take only what's necessary to keep up a decent standard of living," Hannah said curtly. "I never thought I would have a son who would be a miser."

"I'm not a miser, Mama." Fabrice's voice was quite gentle. "But I know the difference between black and red, and unless we can get some pretty good commission before too long we're going to be in the red."

"Nonsense, boy!" Fabrice was fifty, and an elderly fifty, but Hannah still saw him as a boy to be protected and guided. It was something she couldn't help, probably because he was slow and quiet and bumbling in his elderly way, and so utterly different from the fire and restlessness and braggadoccio of Ferdie. He was a throwback to one of her uncles who had been a country squire and bred pigs. Fabrice bred small mechanical things, clocks, watches, musical boxes, antique dolls that curtseyed; or it seemed that he bred them for he persuaded many broken ones to work again. This enchanted Juana, and a very limited clientele. It would be a crime to waste a customer with the potential of Digby Field on Fabrice and his hobby.

"Nonsense," she said again. "I'll be out and about any day now. I'll get things moving. And Patrick must work harder. When did he last make a good purchase? Not since the Renoir. He must forget his exhibition for a little while and contribute to the business. But surely in the meantime we can interest a wealthy customer in more than a clock? Ask him to stay to dinner."

"Tonight?"

"When else? It will balance the table, with Emily Bowman arriving. And if I can't sell him those Flemish tapestries I've lost my touch."

CHAPTER THREE

LUCIE, Patrick's wife, met them in the hall that opened from the courtyard. The cool sound of water splashing gently in the fountain followed them in.

Lucie's high heels clicked sharply on the tiled floor. She was tall and extremely thin. A clothes horse, Emily thought, noticing the smart simplicity of her candy pink suit. She had dark hair casually cut framing a bony face, sallow-skinned, but with beautiful sulky black eyes. She looked very Spanish. Her thinness was elegant, but it gave her hollows in her cheeks and stretched the skin tightly over her cheekbones.

Patrick said, "This is my wife, Lucie."

Emily held out her hand. The cool limp one put in hers

told her at once that Lucie was not welcoming her any more than her husband. She was taken aback. She had imagined from what Patrick had said that Lucie had been enthusiastic about her arrival as an excuse to keep Juana from school.

"I suppose we are cousins," Lucie said in a voice that showed the minimum of interest. "Since I only heard about you for the first time a few weeks ago you do seem to be a stranger. I'll show you your room. Come this way." She began to cross the hall, then went back to speak to her husband.

"Darling, you look quite filthy. Paint all over you, as usual. Do go and clean up. Fabrice has a customer staying to dinner. And Mama's coming down." She lifted her face to kiss Patrick swiftly on the cheek. "Promise to be on your best behaviour tonight. No arguments. Fabrice says Mr. Field is only interested in clocks, but I don't see why he shouldn't be persuaded to buy one of your pictures, too. He's supposed to be rich, and a patron of the arts. I have no objection to being patronised, even if you have."

"My husband is the worst salesman for his own work," she explained to Emily as she came back.

Emily realized that during that small scene Patrick hadn't said a word. He had merely submitted to his wife's kiss.

The quarrel over Juana could not yet have been made up. Lucie was clearly eager for a reconciliation, but Emily's arrival had intensified Patrick's grievance. That, no doubt, was why Lucie's welcome had been so wary.

In the room to which Emily was shown, Lucie remained aloof.

"We have dinner at nine. You'll have time for a bath and a rest. My mother will meet you at dinner. She's been ill and has to avoid excitement, so you'll be careful, won't you?"

"Why should I excite her?" Emily asked.

"I don't see why you should," Lucie said in her clipped voice, "but she has this idea that you're so like her cousin Dolly. She was very devoted to Dolly, and I think she's always been haunted by her death so young. She nursed her, you know, and she couldn't speak Spanish, and I gather it was all pretty dreadful. It might be a bit disturbing for her if you are so like Dolly. But she insisted on your coming, and you try opposing Mama about anything!"

So Lucie had opposed her, in spite of the music lessons for Juana. Why?

"When am I to meet Juana?" Emily asked.

"In the morning. She's had a bad day and thank goodness she's fallen asleep early. She's quite exhausted after one of her turns, poor mite. I'm afraid you were the cause of this one."

"Me!"

"She's nervous of strangers. One of the sisters at the convent where she goes for lessons stupidly rapped her knuckles one day and she's afraid you'll do the same. You will be careful, won't you? She's terribly highly strung and if she's upset she has a convulsion. That's quite terrifying. I've never grown used to them. And then my husband thinks she should be sent off to boarding school, the poor baby. Do children really go to boarding school as young as that in England?"

"Often. Especially boys."

"I think it's heartless." Lucie's fine eyes were flashing. "Why do people have children if they only want to get them out of the way? That's what it is with my husband, you know. He's jealous of the time I give to Juana. He wants me with him much more. He would like me to sit in his studio while he works. I used to when we were first married. But when a baby comes one's life has to change. Doesn't it? Of course you shouldn't know."

"I wouldn't know," Emily returned evenly. "Do you think I could have the shutters open? The air was so beautifully cool outside."

"I suppose so. Tell Maria when she brings up your bags." Belatedly, Lucie asked, "Is there anything else you want? Your bathroom is in there. Mama said you were to have this suite."

Emily looked round the large room with its beautiful furniture and murmured that it was more than a music mistress would normally expect, she was sure.

Lucie had the grace to say, "You are a relation," and turned to go. But again, as downstairs, she had an impulse to come back and say, "You'll see that I'm right when you meet Juana. I believe if she was separated from me she would die."

She stared at Emily aggressively, but there was some hidden torment in her eyes.

"Artists are selfish people," she said. And then, abruptly, she did go.

Emily sat down slowly on the brocade-covered couch at the foot of the bed, and wondered why the possessive love of a man like Patrick Fermoyle should make his wife unhappy.

Presently, with a great clattering, as if she were six people, the little plump Spanish maid, Maria, came in with Emily's bags.

"You wish me to help you unpack, senorita?"

"No, thank you, but open the shutters, please."

Maria was unsurprised. She gave a cheerful grin, and said, "You like plenty of air, senorita? All the English do. *Contemplar!*" She had thrown back the wooden doors and the night air flowed in.

Emily went to the windows and found that her room faced over the courtyard, with its fountain spouting water from four small fat dolphins, and its luxuriating tangle of creepers and vines. A balcony ran round three sides of the courtyard, but all the other windows facing on to the balcony were shuttered. No one else liked air.

"They must be shut in the daytime, senorita," Maria said. "It is very hot, then."

"It's delicious," Emily said, breathing deeply. She stood in the dusk listening to the tinkle of the fountain and wondering whose those shuttered rooms were, which was Cousin Hannah's, which Lucie's and Patrick's, which Juana's. She was a little surprised and impatient with herself for feeling so involved already with this family. It was scarcely because of the blood tie. It must be because of a subconscious desire to escape her own troubles. It was always easier to find solutions for other people's. So should she proceed to take the troublesome Juana off her mother's hands, so that Lucie could go back to her habit of sitting in Patrick's studio while he worked?

She shrugged, thinking that it wasn't a very exciting role for herself. She was quite sure that the lovely Dolly, taking her first breaths of the jasmine-scented air, hadn't had any such unselfish motives. She had probably been dreaming already of the man she had fallen in love with, or was about to fall in love with.

Dolly had no prerogative on love. Perhaps Emily would repeat her story, only without a Hannah to kill her dream, without pain and death. "Love!" her teacher, darling Victor, had said, dismissing it as an awkward untidy and time-stealing emotion. "That must wait until you have established your career." So she had agreed to the fierce discipline, the complete involvement that music required. But now she was free, she had all the time in the world to lavish on that awkward, untidy, and ravishing emotion.

When Emily went back into her room Maria had gone, but she had disregarded Emily's instructions and unpacked. She must have done it quickly for all Emily's dresses were hanging in the wardrobe, a nightgown spread out on her bed, her cosmetics neatly arranged on the dressing-table.

This was Dolly Bowman treatment, not strictly meant for Emily Bowman who was reduced to being a music teacher. Nevertheless, it was very pleasant, and Emily sang softly as she ran water into the big marble bath. She would wear the red silk sheath, she decided. She wouldn't look like a music teacher, either tonight or at any unnecessary time.

Dripping with the refreshing water that had washed away all the travel dust she rubbed herself with the big white towel, and shrugged into her *négligée*.

She clutched it sharply round herself when she saw the big woman standing in her room.

"Excuse me, miss, I thought you said come in."

Emily was almost certain there had been no knock. However, invited or not, there the intruder was, not tall but very broad in her black dress and spotless white apron and cap.

"The mistress sent me to see if you have everything you need, miss."

"Why!" Emily cried in excited recognition. "You must be Patterson. Daddy said as far as he knew you were still here. I'm so glad to meet you."

"That's very kind of you, miss, though I don't know why you should be glad to meet me. It's the mistress who's anxious to see you."

But Patterson, in spite of her correct voice (she must have been well-trained in the days when servants were really servants, and goodness, Cousin Hannah was lucky to have such a faithful retainer), couldn't quite conceal her own interest. Her flat grey eyes were not missing anything of Emily's appearance. She looked faintly shocked, Emily thought. Perhaps because Emily had rushed out of the bathroom bare-footed and half-clad, her hair tumbling down from its casual twist on top of her head, her face already damp again from the muggy heat. Dolly, she supposed, had never shown herself half-clad to anyone, and much less Cousin Hannah, from the sound of her.

"But I *am* glad to see you, Patterson. You're my first link with my legendary Aunt Dolly. There's so much I want to know about her."

"Such as what, miss?"

Was there the faintest hostility in the woman's voice? Was she jealous about her ghost?

"Well, how she looked, for instance."

"Your mirror can tell you that, miss."

Emily spun round to look at her reflection in the lovely old silver-framed mirror over the dressing-table. She pushed up her tumbling hair.

"Am I so much like her, Patterson?"

"You gave me quite a turn when I saw you, miss. I'll have to warn the mistress. I expect Miss Lucie told you her health has been poor. The doctor has ordered a very quiet life, but will she take heed? She worries us all to death. Tomorrow, if you please, she intends to take flowers to the cemetery as usual."

"For—"

"For her late husband," Patterson said primly, after the smallest deliberate silence. And again Emily had a feeling that Patterson was showing not so much hostility as a hidden ironic amusement.

Patterson's many years of repression had flowered into something, after all. One was not surprised, considering first Dolly's wilfulness and then so many years of Hannah's autocracy. What was it behind her placid face, her mouth turned up for laughter? Just the amusement of the onlooker?

It had seemed that she had been going to laugh because Emily had thought the flowers were to be for Dolly's grave.

"Then everything's all right, miss? I can tell the mistress you'll be down at a quarter to nine. She likes punctuality."

"Yes, Patterson, I'll be down. Oh, and Patterson," she couldn't help adding impulsively, "do tell her how excited I am to be here. It was so terribly kind of her to ask me, a complete stranger, just because I had had some trouble."

"Not such a stranger, miss," Patterson said, and chuckled a little as she waddled out. Her chuckle was asthmatic, and cosy, and sounded as if it came easily to the fat woman.

All the same, Emily knew that she hadn't formed the faintest clue what Patterson was really feeling about her arrival. Neither Lucie nor Patrick had been pleased to see her, and now this elderly woman was enigmatic and somehow extremely secretive.

But although very much a part of the household, she was only a maid, and surely didn't need to be worried about.

And you, said Emily vigorously to her reflection in the mirror, aren't a ghost, and had better not find yourself being treated as one. No dead woman's shoes for you, my girl. A new life for you in this glorious sunshine. Love, living, fun, freedom. . . . All the things poor unlucky Dolly lost so soon.

It was half an hour later, just before she was ready to go downstairs, that the child began screaming.

The sound came from the room next to Emily's, and was so full of terror and urgency that she dropped her hair-brush and ran into the passage to see what was happening. When nobody came, and the high-pitched frenzied screams continued, she opened the door from behind which the sounds came, and found herself in the child's bedroom.

The child Juana.

A nightlight was burning on the bedside table. Its frail circle of light showed the little girl sitting upright, her last scream arrested as Emily came in.

She certainly looked a forlorn little creature, with wisps of blonde hair sticking to her hot face, her pale blue eyes distended until they seemed to be all whites. She was painfully thin, too, her bird-bone arms hugged across her narrow chest.

"You're Juana," said Emily.

The child stared, her mouth hanging open. Emily was reassured that there was nothing too much wrong, since surprise could stop the painful screams. She remembered Patrick's words that his daughter had screaming fits at the slightest provocation. She didn't look very much like the child of that virile man, except for her blondeness which didn't come from her mother. Indeed, she looked like a portrait of one of those over-bred delicate princesses with tendencies to lung disease or anaemia, anxious, solemn little creatures with the weight of brocade on their narrow shoulders and the weight of destiny on their heads. Juana could be no child of destiny. She was more likely a pawn between highly individual parents. Her father was jealous of her, her mother smothered her with love. So she had nightmares and woke screaming.

"I'm your cousin Emily," Emily went on calmly. 'That

was a terrible noise you were making. What was it all about?"

The distressed pink was going out of the child's face leaving it papery white. It was true that she looked alarmingly delicate. The pale almost invisible eyebrows and eyelashes added to her colorlessness. She looked petulant, peevish, intelligent, and yet touchingly innocent. It was not an unprepossessing face for all its plainness.

"I was frightened," she whispered at last in answer to Emily's question.

"Why?"

"I woke up and there was nobody here. I want my mother."

Emily sat on the bed. "Won't I do?"

"No."

"But why not? We have to get to know each other."

The child made a petulant movement.

"I'm nervous of strangers."

"That sounds parrot talk to me. And, anyway, I'm not a stranger, I'm your cousin. You have a pretty name. Juana. There was a queen of Spain called that, did you know? Queen Juana." Without thinking, Emily added the popular appellation, "Juana la loca."

Instantaneously the child was as rigid as a poker and screaming, "Don't call me that! Don't call me that!"

"Why, goodness, I told you Juana was a queen."

"La Loca was not! She was not! She's a dirty old woman. She makes a noise like leaves rustling. I know she's there even when Maria says she isn't. I won't be like her! I hate you for saying that!"

Juana had punctuated this breathless statement with screams, and now fell back on the pillow, her small face an alarming bluish color. Emily was bending over her anxiously when Lucie rushed in.

"What's happening? Did you upset her?" Lucie had gathered the small body in her arms, and with relief Emily saw that it was losing its rigidity. The child, acting or not, had had her scared.

"I came in because she screamed. I thought she'd had a nightmare. We were talking quite nicely until I seemed to say the wrong thing."

Rocking her backwards and forwards and murmuring, "There, precious! You're better now. Mama's here. Nothing's going to frighten you," Lucie stared at Emily with brilliant undisguisedly hostile eyes. "What exactly did you say?"

"I really don't know," Emily said bewilderedly, "I was talking about the Spanish queen, Juana, and she began screaming that she wouldn't be like La Loca."

"I should think you did say the wrong thing. La Loca's an—No, darling, we're not going to talk about her. I promise. Anyway, haven't I told you again and again there's no one in that house? Did Maria take you walking that way? If she did, I'll be very angry with her."

The child shook her head violently.

"No, she didn't. She didn't, she didn't, she didn't."

"She's going to take ages to calm down," Lucie said coldly to Emily. "You might ring for Maria and tell her to bring up some hot milk."

Emily could see that she was to be the scapegoat for this latest of Juana's frequent scenes. No doubt there always was a scapegoat so that the child was never made to face her fantasies and fears. She shrugged very slightly. It was a pity to have walked into trouble so early, but at least she knew now what she had to cope with. Half Juana's hysterical scenes, as her father had said, were self-induced, but the other half could well come from sheer terror. That wasn't a thing you could run away from. You had to pick up a sword and slay the child's dragons.

CHAPTER FOUR

HANNAH had come downstairs half an hour before anyone else so as to give herself time to recover from the exercise. Patterson knew this very well. There had never been any use in trying to hide anything from Patterson, but one could still try to preserve one's dignity before other people.

By the time everyone came into the big cool room her heart would have stopped its inconvenient fluttering and she would be sitting as composed and commanding as always in the straight-backed tapestry-covered chair with its elaborately carved arms and legs. The chair had come, she had been told, from a cardinal's palace. It pleased her to sit her irreligious body where a prince of the church had once sat.

She was able to sit perfectly still and relaxed, a discipline that fifty years ago she had drummed into the ears of her small pupils, until the others began to come in.

She greeted them pleasantly, Lucie in her candy pink suit that looked expensive but not as expensive as it had actually been, Patrick tidied up, his hair brushed and glistening, his hands innocent of paint.

Privately Hannah thought Patrick much more interesting in his working clothes, but even this gesture towards civilized living couldn't take away his individuality, his curbed forcefulness, the feeling he gave one of being able in the right circumstances to live with intense infectious enthusiasm. He didn't seem to find those circumstances in this house. But why not, Hannah thought querulously. He had so much more than he had ever had. Lucie should have been an attractive and satisfying wife. Wasn't she clever enough? Why was it the woman who always had to be so clever, scheming to hold a man? Even Dolly, who had imagined herself invincible in those matters, had had to face the harsh truth.

"I suppose he was only intrigued for a little while by my fair hair and blue eyes. But he wants his wife to be sultry and dark and Spanish. Do you think that's what it is, Hannah?"

"I expect so." Hannah could hear her own dogged voice. *"A family like his doesn't marry outside their own kind. . ."*

Had Patrick, in marrying Lucie, half Spanish and inclined to moodiness and awkward displays of temperament, married outside his own kind, and was trying to make the best of it? Perhaps. She must see that something like that didn't happen to Emily. Emily! She longed to talk about her.

"Did you have any difficulty in identifying her?" she asked Patrick. "Did she look the way you expected her to?"

"She hardly looked like a music mistress," said Patrick evasively. He asked Hannah if she would have a drink and she said she would have mineral water. Lucie wanted a Campari and soda. Hannah noticed that the pulse was jumping in Patrick's cheek, a sure sign of tension. He and Lucie must have quarrelled again.

"Why all this fuss for a music teacher, Mama?" Lucie asked.

"Fuss?" Hannah preferred not to notice the slight touch

of jealousy in Lucie's voice. It was becoming too frequent. She was even jealous, now, when people noticed Juana. And few enough people did, poor little scrap.

"Look at you, dressed for a grand party."

"Ah!" Hannah patted her skirt in a satisfied way. "I'm glad you noticed. But you're wrong as to the reason. This is for Fabrice's guest. We must make a suitable impression."

"If you make that sort of impression, Mamita," said Patrick, "he'll think you don't need to sell anything, not even a snuff box."

It pleased her when Patrick called her Mamita. Like all quick-tempered men he had a disarming tenderness. She wondered how often Lucie saw it. It was her own fault if she didn't.

"One must never be in the position of the supplicant," she said. "It weakens one's position. Ah, here is Fabrice, and—" She half rose as Fabrice brought the stranger forward.

"This is Mr. Field, Mama. My mother, Mr. Field. She's recovering from an illness, as I told you."

Hannah shot one of her glaring topaz glances at Fabrice.

"I am not recovering, I have recovered. How do you do, Mr. Field? I hear you are a collector."

"Yes, I have a few things. My father made money out of buying slums so I like to balance the ledger by buying works of art."

That was honesty. It pleased Hannah, making her glow expansive.

"How wise. Most collectors are over sixty and can't tell a Fragonard from a picture calendar. Not because they haven't the knowledge but because their eyesight isn't good enough any longer." She cackled with pleasure. She was beginning to enjoy herself. Out of her sickroom at last and into the fray. This young man Fabrice had produced looked interesting, cool and shrewd and knowledgeable. She'd sell him those Flemish tapestries before the night was over, and so start retrieving a situation that had been getting alarmingly out of hand.

"Mama, you're surely not drinking!" Fabrice was saying worriedly in her ear.

"Taste it," she ordered, thrusting the glass at him. "It will have you under the table in two swallows. Mineral water! To think I've come to that." In a lower voice she said, "What does he want?"

"I told you, Mama. He collects clocks. Unfortunately he wants a Tompion and I haven't got one."

Fabrice was looking flurried and hot, his large black eyes a little bloodshot and restless. He always got that harried look with customers. He was strictly a backroom boy. Hannah secretly attributed this to his Spanish blood. He had inherited all the lethargic qualities of a race that lived in a hot country, and none of the restlessness and drive that Ferdie had had.

"Then you must find him one, mustn't you?"

"I've promised to do my best. It's possible I can get one from—" Fabrice's voice died away as the door opened and Dolly walked in.

But it wasn't Dolly, of course. Such a flood of heat had swept over Hannah that for a moment she couldn't think properly.

Dolly would never have worn that short crimson dress.

But yes, she would if she had been a young girl today. It was just the kind of thing she would have worn, though she had never needed to dress up her startling beauty.

She had liked to cause a stir of interest when she walked into a room, and this girl with her slim body and long legs and high crown of blonde hair was obviously exactly the same. With complete self-possession she crossed the room and bent to kiss Hannah on each cheek. Hannah's skin contracted beneath the soft young lips.

"Cousin Hannah, I'm so happy to meet you. It was so good of you to ask me here. Lucie and Patterson said you were ill, but you're looking fabulous."

The warmth swept over Hannah again. She took one of Emily's hands in both of her own old dry ones, the rings, Ferdie's modest diamond, and Dolly's huge aquamarine, glinting in sharp contrast to the brown wrinkled skin.

"I've quite recovered from a very unimportant illness. Everyone fusses far too much. I'm so glad to see you, my child. I hope you had a good journey. But I mustn't monopolise you now. Later we'll talk. I want to know about you and your family, especially your father. Does he still think I put poison in Dolly's tea?" She cackled gently. "I believe he always thought that, but it was the Italians, not the Spaniards, who were the great poisoners. A pity. I always had a fondness for the poisoned glove. Fabrice! Come and meet Emily. And bring Mr. Field. Emily, this is Mr.

Field from London. He wants to buy a clock, but I intend to sell him some tapestries instead."

"Are they from Goya cartoons?" Mr. Field asked interestedly.

"Regrettably, no. But they're very beautiful, all the same."

"No one told me I should find anything as beautiful as this here," said Mr. Field, his admiring eyes on Emily.

Emily laughed, and Hannah's unreliable heart gave another jump. That disarming naïve pleasure at a compliment was Dolly over again. And there were all the men looking at Emily, as men had always looked at Dolly. Even Patrick, as if he hadn't made her acquaintance an hour ago, as if already he couldn't take his eyes off her.

Fear stirred in Hannah as the voices and pictures momentarily took possession of her again.

Dolly under the lemon tree in the far corner of the garden saying with a brief return of her old gay confidence, "But you know men always made such fools of themselves over me, Hannah. I had to literally drive them away. That's why I get this feeling that something must have happened to Jaime, some accident. What's that you've got in your hand?"

Hannah held out the column torn from the newspaper. Even in her limited Spanish she could read that among the spectators at the famous bull-ring in Seville had been Don Jaime Pestoza of Toledo. He had watched the great El Burgos . . .

Dolly let the paper flutter from her hand. She picked up her sewing again, the fine lawn that she had said she would make into a gown for Hannah's baby. But her fingers trembled too much to insert the needle. She could no longer go on deceiving herself that it was some terrible accident that had kept Jaime away.

"You don't believe he ever loved me, do you, Hannah?"

"How should I know?" Hannah said roughly. "I don't pretend to understand the Spanish temperament. I don't even understand my own husband half the time."

"I understood it," Dolly said dreamily. "Perfectly."

Then suddenly she threw down her sewing, crying passionately, "He did love me. I know he did. But now no one does. Except Patterson."

"Patterson!" said Hannah contemptuously.

"Why not? Servants can have emotions as well as us. And who else has she got to love?" Dolly's extraordinarily pure and honest eyes scorned Hannah. What maid, no matter

how anxious to expend emotions, would make Hannah the object of her devotion? Besides, Hannah was married. She had Ferdie.

It was natural that Dolly and Patterson should draw together. They were the same age, they had travelled together, Patterson had watched and sympathised with all Dolly's excitements and tribulations.

"Patterson will love me," Dolly said wistfully. "And perhaps your baby will, Hannah. I hope it's a girl. I'd like it to be a girl. . . ."

And here, in a strange way, Hannah realized dazedly, was that girl. Staring at Emily she wondered, with apprehension, what she had unleashed in this house? A ghost, with all that trouble to live over again?

The scene shifted and clarified. Lucie began talking animatedly to Patrick, claiming his attention. Mr. Field, remembering his good manners, began a conversation about the tapestries in the Escorial, and Hannah heard Fabrice politely hoping that Emily would enjoy her stay in Granada. The queerly nasty little spell was broken.

To Emily, the evening that followed was sharp and exciting. It should have been dreamlike with these fascinating people, but she was too acutely alive and aware to be in a dream. There was Lucie, elegant and animated, entertaining Mr. Field. There was Patrick, less picturesque in formal clothes, but not entirely tamed, for a spark of impatience still glinted in his eyes. Fabrice, bumbling, over-weight, lugubrious, and shy. And Hannah, fabulous, like an old bejewelled lizard blinking in the light. Hannah, picturesque as Dolly, for all her beauty, could never have been.

Emily longed for her father to see Hannah. He would be as surprised and delighted as she was. Hannah the Governess in black bombasine turning into this elegant Spanish lady in that wonderful mantilla the colour of smoke, and the superb violet gown that was most certainly *haute couture*.

Indeed, Emily would be surprised if there was anything fake in the whole house. The table silver was Georgian, the wine glasses antique Bohemian crystal, the dinner service a Meissen set that had belonged to a Viennese archduchess, the table-cloth Brussels lace. Fabrice had whispered this information to her and added that the house with its contents was their shop window.

"We sell off stuff now and again when Mama can be persuaded to part with it. One thing I'll never separate her from is her bed. She lies in it imagining she's one of the old Spanish queens, I shouldn't be surprised."

"But you surely won't ever have to sell it," Emily said.

Fabrice looked uneasy. "We're in business, after all." Then he added, "At least, not while she's alive." And seemed relieved when Lucie claimed his attention.

This gave Emily the opportunity to talk to Patrick on her other side. He had been disappointingly uncommunicative when she had asked him about his work. She had thought that the civilized atmosphere might have banished his aloofness. But although he was outwardly conforming to the required good behaviour, his taut explosive look was even more apparent, as if Hannah's cherished Bohemian crystal or even the gold-edged dinner plates might not be entirely safe within his reach. For some reason, he was simply enduring this occasion. That made her wonder if every evening here was the same for him, something to be endured. That would be terrible. She was catching his tension as much as she had caught his daughter's earlier. That made her say, "I've met Juana. Not very successfully, I'm afraid."

"Did she behave badly?"

"Not exactly. But what is she frightened of?"

"Juana? Frightened?"

You should know, Emily thought, you're her father.

"I think that's why she has these screaming fits."

"Don't be fooled, Miss Bowman. She screams to get attention."

"Call me Emily, for goodness' sake! I am practically your cousin." She added, "I wouldn't have thought you were a man who would be slow to use a girl's name," and got what she had intended, a sharp scrutiny from eyes that were curious now, but still refusing to be friendly.

"Am I to be psycho-analyzed now?"

"No, you're not. But you haven't answered my question. What is Juana frightened of? I'm sure it isn't my imagination that she has something on her mind that terrifies her."

"Oh, she has nightmares. That's true enough."

"About an old woman?"

"Not that again!"

"Someone called La Loca? A dirty old woman who makes a noise like leaves rustling."

"She imagines it," Patrick said. "She got a fright once when one of the maids took her walking past a house in the Calle de Fatima. It belongs to some rich Spaniard, but he hasn't been near it for years and the garden's overgrown, vines climbing all over the place. The house is empty except for caretakers. If you care for that sort of thing, there's a story that some previous owner of the house shut up his wife in one of the rooms for unfaithfulness. She was supposed to have been kept there for several years and finally died of weeping." His sceptical eyes were on her. "Do you think any woman could weep that much?"

"Perhaps," said Emily. "So the house is haunted by this poor tear-drowned ghost?"

"Something like that. There's supposed to be an old woman with wild hair who appears at the upstairs windows. She's called La Loca, the mad woman. Unfortunately a silly maid we had told Juana the story and she's had these nightmares ever since. The maids have been told never to take her past the house, but you can't be sure they'll obey. The street's near the Generalife Gardens where they go to meet their boy friends."

"What a fascinating story. No wonder Juana was terrified. You should understand how a child can be haunted. Didn't you have some private bogey?"

"Plenty of them."

"And didn't your mother comfort you?"

"My mother died when I was six. I can hardly remember her."

"I'm sorry. That must have been awful. Then how were you brought up?"

He laughed. "In the art galleries of Europe. My father wanted to be a successful painter, but he took an easier way, he drank instead. He'd park me in the Louvre or the Rijksmuseum, or the Prado, and go off to the nearest pub. I studied Velazquez and Vermeer and he studied Johnnie Walker. But don't get me wrong. He was charming, extrovert, terribly amusing. An eternal optimist. I loved him. He died after falling into a canal in Venice. And he gave me quite an inheritance. The determination to do something, to be something. On top of this, I was the best-informed child on art in Europe. Ask me anything about any great painting . . . Well, never mind. We were talking about Juana. I don't want her to know that sort of loneliness. It's what bogeys, as you call them, thrive on."

"I can help," Emily murmured. She was quite suddenly noticing what good hands he had, strong, long-fingered, articulate. And strangely naked without those traces of paint.

"You can help, sure, but you're not her age. She isn't her own age herself. She's either precociously adult or a baby. She's got to learn to be a child with other children."

"Yes, I suppose you're right. Although it's true, as her mother says, that she looks terribly delicate."

"She'll grow out of that."

"You do love her," Emily said.

"Did you think I didn't?"

"I thought you might hate her."

He grinned. Suddenly he looked much younger.

"I can do that, too." He drained his glass. "Have I talked too much? It's the wine. But it's necessary in this house. You'll find out."

He was looking at her now as if he really saw her. It was an impersonal appraisal, his eyes cool and candid, but Emily knew that, temporarily, anyway, he had stopped thinking of her as a strange female brought in to cope with his daughter, and as such an unwelcome intruder. Now he was scrutinising her as he might have done a girl who had caught his attention in the street or in a café. Someone who simply pleased him visually. At least she was hoping with some intensity that she pleased him.

"Who told you to wear red?" he asked.

"I have a mind of my own."

"I'd like to see you in yellow. Dark honey." He looked at her for so long that she grew uncomfortable. Then he said absently, "I can never get my wife out of pink. She thinks it has an irresistible appeal to men."

To men? Or to her husband? Emily looked across at Lucie, and realized, with some confusion, that she and Patrick had been ignoring the others for much too long. For the first time she was aware of tiredness. It had been an exhilarating but exhausting day. She had come a very long way.

"What have you two been talking about?" Lucie asked in her quick brittle voice.

"The sad story of my life," said Patrick.

"Poor Emily. She must be in tears. What do you think, Mr. Field?"

"I don't know your husband's life, Mrs. Fermoyle. Is it something to weep about?"

Everyone laughed. But somehow that remark had ended the dinner party. Hannah began to rise, tightening her mouth as she had to wait for Fabrice's help.

She said in her autocratic voice, "Mr. Field, come and see these tapestries," and as soon as she had got her balance completely, slowly, with the aid of her stick, walked out of the room, followed by the Englishman.

Emily heard Lucie saying swiftly to Patrick, "Darling, I've told him about your exhibition. He's interested."

"What else could the poor devil say? Sitting there eating our food."

"Oh, for heaven's sake, what do you expect me to do? Pretend you're above making money?"

"I won't have people snared in this way. I've told you before. I'd rather sell my pictures on the sidewalk."

"Are you interested in clocks?" Emily started at Fabrice's voice in her ear. "Would you like to come and see my collection tomorrow?"

"Very much," Emily said, still straining her ears to hear what Patrick and Lucie were saying.

"I have some interesting musical boxes, too. Some of them were hopelessly broken when I got them but I've made them all work again. Juana likes them, although she likes the clockwork dolls better."

"Dolls?"

"I can see that you're thinking like Mama that I have childish tastes."

"They sound very nice tastes," Emily said, suddenly drawn to this plump middle-aged man with the anxious eyes. He was so unlike any son one would have expected Hannah to have that he, too, must have his forms of loneliness.

"But not extremely profitable," came his apologetic voice. "It's a great disappointment to my mother. I'm a throwback to some rustic uncles, apparently. Just as you are to Dolly."

"How do you know I am?" Emily demanded. "You can't have seen her. Or if you did you must have been just a baby."

"No, I don't remember seeing her, that's true. I'm only going by what my mother says. She's astonished at the resemblance. She was very devoted to Dolly, you know."

"I thought she was jealous of her. That's what my father said."

"No, no, she nearly lost her life for Dolly. She nursed her through typhus, and caught it herself. That's devotion for you."

There was no time to say more, for Hannah had come back with Mr. Field. She was saying testily, "Of course I admit that your eyesight is better than mine. It ought to be since I'm seventy-five years old. But I can't agree I'm a hundred years out in dating those tapestries. I'll get another opinion."

"That's very sensible," said Mr. Field. "I'll be happy to be proved wrong. May I give you my London address? I'll be glad to hear from you if you turn up anything interesting."

The evening was over. Hannah thought she would never reach her room, never survive the ordeal of undressing. She had wanted a good piece of business so badly, as much to prove that she was still alive and functioning as for the money. She had neglected her old finesse and practically dragged the Englishman, Mr. Field, in by the short hairs. And what had happened? He had bluntly let her know that she had made another mistake.

"I told you you were mad to go down, madam," came Patterson's righteous voice. "Now look at you. A wet rag. And I hear you've made a mistake about those tapestries."

"Is there anything in this house you don't hear, Patterson?"

"Where it concerns you, madam, I doubt it. Your interests have always been mine."

"Well, don't sound so smug about it! Yes, if you must know, I have made another mistake." Hannah's voice was petulant, appealing. She had to pull herself up sharply. Before she knew it she would be asking Patterson for pity. That would never do. One had to go on presenting an unbroken front, otherwise she knew instinctively that she would crumble, show her deathly tiredness. . . .

All the same, the evening had by no means been all disaster. That girl. The charm of her. She had burst into the room like a jacaranda flower. Naughtily, seductively, dressed just like Dolly. Innocently pleased with her own attractiveness. There was innocence there, at least. It must be cherished. It was a rare quality in this house.

Hannah sat at the window breathing in the cool air, trying to recover a little strength. Mad, Patterson had said. It was a word she had been using too much lately.

"You can't afford many more of those botches, madam."

"Don't go on about it, Patterson. Anyway, I've made no botch, as you so picturesquely call it, about Emily. She's Dolly all over again."

"Is that a good thing, Madam?"

"*I* think it is," Hannah said stoutly.

But her confidence had been shaken by Digby Field and yet one more expensive mistake. She had paid too much for those tapestries. Now she was developing other fears. And the clamouring voices were in her head again.

"Dolly, aren't you ever going to stop mooning over that man? You'll make yourself ill. You look ill already, as white as paper. And your eyes. If only you could see them. They look—"

Dolly's hands were in front of her eyes, protectively.

"How do they look? Mad?"

The question was shot at Hannah who had to laugh quickly and reassuringly.

"Of course not. But not—really not quite natural. Your mother always said you were too highly strung. You used to be in floods of tears after your parties. I'm sure I'd never have cried if I could have had a party."

"Oh, Hannah, why will you go on and on, saying I always had everything? You don't need to any longer. It's the other way round now. You have the husband, the b-baby . . . Hannah!" The beseeching hands clutched at Hannah's wrists. "Did anyone tell him something about me? I mean, about my being too highly strung, or that I was delicate?"

"Who could, silly goose?" said Hannah. "There's only me here, and I couldn't even speak Spanish. . . ."

Hannah said slowly, reluctantly, "Supposing *he* came to Granada."

Patterson's placid expression didn't change. "Does he ever?"

"I don't think so. People say not."

"Then why would he now?"

"It's unlikely, I suppose. But if he saw her he'd recognize her at once. He couldn't help it."

"And think himself mad?" Patterson said cryptically. She had her back turned and didn't see Hannah's sharp shudder. "Aren't you ever going to bed, madam?"

Hannah cast a sideways look at the bed and wondered if she could reach it without Patterson's help. She noticed that from where she sat she was reflected in the Florentine mirror: an old woman, an old, old woman like a shrivelled leaf ready to drop off its tree. She was no longer invulnerable, no longer everlasting. And no longer infallible.

"All right, I'm coming to bed," she said irascibly. "And don't forget to order the flowers for the cemetery tomorrow."

CHAPTER FIVE

THERE were flowers everywhere, cascading over the balcony, flourishing in pots on windowsills and in every corner of the courtyard, not to count the enormous bouquet of carnations and roses wrapped in cellophane, which arrived during the morning. But they were quickly whisked away by Patterson who took them upstairs to Cousin Hannah's room.

Emily thought that probably last night's guest, Mr. Field, had sent them.

She had breakfasted alone, which had disappointed her, because she was longing to talk to someone. But apparently Patrick had eaten early and gone to work in his studio, Fabrice was not yet down, and Lucie and Hannah both had breakfast in their rooms. She hadn't seen a sign of Juana, but was told she was with her mother and would be brought down later for her first lesson at the piano. The maid, Maria, the plump girl with bold brilliant black eyes, was more than ready to gossip. She spoke excellent English. But Concita, the young shy creature who brought Emily her rolls and coffee, couldn't be persuaded to say a word except, *"Bueno dias, senorita."* Nevertheless, when she returned to the kitchen there was immediately a clatter of voices. The Spanish were a vociferous race. Their cheerful chatter had sounded since dawn.

Fabrice eventually came in. He was pleasantly friendly, although his plump face had a pouched creased look as if he had slept badly. He was the only one of this family apart from Hannah who behaved as if she were a welcome guest. Already Emily looked on him with affection.

"Well, Emily. How was your first night in Granada?"

"Wonderful."

"Not too hot?"

"No, I slept with the shutters open, and this morning the air was so sparkling and bright I couldn't think why anyone ever lived in England."

"Wait till later in the day. Unless you're one of those people who thrive on heat. Mama is. She soaks it up like a lizard. It kills me. I guess I'm too fat. When are you coming to see my clocks?"

"As soon as I can."

"Come this afternoon. We close between one o'clock and four for siesta time. But I'll be in my workroom. That's when I get the real work done, though Mama wouldn't agree."

"What's the shop like?"

"Oh, don't expect too much of that. It's quite small. We only show a few pictures and a bit of bric-à-brac. We do our real business here. Or Mama does. We have clients we buy for privately, or at auctions. Someone wants a Goya, we do our best to find one for sale."

"Something as important as that," Emily said in admiration.

Fabrice shook his head resignedly.

"I don't have the nerve for it, or the eye for that matter. Mama had. Nerves of iron and a wonderful intuition. She and my father used to go to all the famous auction sales. But ten years ago my father died, and I was no good at it, I was much happier with the little things. And now Mama's got old and her eyesight's failing, and she's made some very expensive mistakes. So the Bowman Galleries aren't what they were." Again Fabrice shook his big head sadly. "Not that I mind. I like my own small business. But there's this house to keep up. As you can see, we've been used to living like lords. And it breaks Mama's heart to part with a thing. The Renoir went a few weeks ago, and it was immediately after that that she had her illness. She and my father had bought it years ago, against a rainy day. It never rains in Spain, they say." Fabrice laughed hollowly. "The Renoir wasn't a good one, it was very small. But it fetched enough to run the house for a few months, and that was what it had been intended for, as I kept pointing out to Mama. She wouldn't see it, she said it was a little piece of her heart being broken off and sold. She and Papa had bought it together, and so on. So you see, if we're to sell any of her other treasures it might well kill her. She's just not reasonable the way she used to be. She says beautiful things around her are necessary to her spirit, because she was deprived of them in her youth. Can't we wait to sell them until she's in her grave?

"Not only that," Fabrice went on, gloomily refilling his coffee cup, "but she's brought Lucie up to want the best, too. The two of them spend enough on clothes alone to keep the average Spanish family for several years."

"But doesn't Lucie's husband—doesn't Patrick support his wife?"

"In Paris gowns? Patrick's a struggling artist. He came into the shop one day to see if we'd show some of his pictures, Mama brought him home to dinner, he met Lucie—and there it was. And I have to say he's useful, he's an expert on pictures. But how many artists can buy their wives Balenciaga gowns? Tell me that."

"And Lucie still insists on them!" Emily said, shocked.

"A man in love will do anything," Fabrice said disgustedly. "Or try to. So one way and another—I care about my family," he said, burying his face in his cup.

"How extraordinary!" Emily murmured.

He lifted his lugubrious gaze. He looked a little like a melancholy bloodhound, his large Spanish eyes enormous and perplexed.

"That I should care about my family? Don't they do that in England?"

"No, I didn't mean that," Emily said quickly. "I meant that Cousin Hannah has grown exactly like my Aunt Dolly used to be. Extravagant and reckless. And she was the one who used to condemn Dolly. Or so my father said."

"Then I suppose it runs in the family," said Fabrice gloomily. "The next thing, Juana will be wanting real pearls."

Emily wanted to comfort him, he looked so lugubrious. "Aren't you worrying too much? Things turn up all the time. This Mr. Field last night might be a good customer. You'll find him the clock he wants. Surely there'll be other things."

Fabrice gave his slow smile. "You're quite right, Emily. And I shouldn't be burdening you with all my worries like this. You're too sympathetic. There's something in your face that makes me talk too much."

"Perhaps I can help. I'd like to. Your mother's already helped me enormously. I wasn't very happy myself a few weeks ago. But one door closes and another opens, at least it does if there's someone like Cousin Hannah about."

"She can be an old monster," Fabrice said indulgently. "You'll find out. Well, perhaps you can help, who knows? Anyway, you shall inspect my clocks precisely at two o'clock this afternoon. Agreed?"

"Agreed," said Emily, laughing.

Patrick didn't put in an appearance. Emily, wandering about restlessly, wanted to go to his studio and ask to see his work, but was afraid she would be unwelcome. She must be polite and wait for an invitation. Probably Lucie would take the opportunity to be with him when she took over Juana for her first piano lesson.

It wasn't until eleven o'clock that Lucie said Juana was ready. Then it seemed that she spoke with the intention of keeping Emily rather than her small daughter occupied.

Juana, however, had disappeared. Maria said the *nina* had gone out into the garden and was probably hiding in the maze, a favorite habit of hers when she was wanted.

Emily hadn't known there was a maze, and said that she would like to see it. She would find Juana and bring her in.

The maze, constructed out of privet bushes growing densely together and six feet high, was surrounded by a high stone wall covered with vines and morning glory. There were orange trees bearing fruit that hung like small yellow moons, and a silver grey olive, its branches gnarled and twisted. There were acacias and rose bushes, and a stunted pomegranate. The garden was a green refuge from the now blazing sun.

Juana was not to be seen, but when Emily called she heard a high-pitched giggle close at hand. It was absurd that such a small maze should be so baffling. Each time she turned a corner, expecting to see the pink of Juana's frock, there was nothing but the pebbled path and perhaps a small bird darting away.

"Juana!" called Lucie from the courtyard. "Come, darling. Don't be naughty."

Juana's excited giggle, just on the verge of hysteria, was so close that Emily opened her mouth to say, "It's all right, I've caught her," and, laughing already, cannoned into Patrick's arms.

For one moment she didn't know what had happened, and she didn't think he did, either. A branch had caught a strand of her hair and let it fall into her eyes. She brushed it aside, and saw him looking down into her hot face. His eyes were as blue as the blazing sky, and the glitter in them certainly was not anger. He had caught her firmly round the waist. She could still feel his hands against the cage of her ribs after he had abruptly let them fall.

"Where's that devil of a child?" he said. And then, "I hope I didn't hurt you."

"Of course not. I was practically on Juana's heels when——"

"Juana's here," called Lucie. "What are you two doing?"

Juana was clinging to her mother's skirts, her expression half fearful, half defiant. It was lucky she was there to take everybody's attention, for Emily's heart was hammering in a most peculiar way, and she had caught a fleeting expression on Lucie's face that had nothing to do with maternal concern. It had looked remarkably like hatred. For her? But Lucie scarcely knew her. Then for Patrick?

"If she's to have music lessons," said Patrick quite mildly, "wouldn't it be better to have them without these complications?"

"It's only nervousness," said Lucie placatingly. "Don't scold her. You know what will happen if you do."

"Then let Emily take her and get started. I'm sure Emily doesn't want to waste her time playing hide and seek each morning."

Lucie dropped her head over Juana's tousled blonde one. "Emily has plenty of time to waste. Hasn't she, love? All the same, I think it might be a good idea to begin, otherwise you won't be finished by lunchtime. Run along with Emily, that's a pet."

Juana clung tighter to her mother, and shuffled her feet preparatory to stamping them.

"You come, too, Mummy. I want you, too."

"Juana!" Patrick's voice had lost its patience. "Go with Emily at once. You don't need your mother. What do you think Emily is going to do? Eat you?"

"Patrick! You know she's worse if you shout at her."

"Then what am I to do? Stand by silently while my eight-year-old daughter goes on being a baby? Is she to be a baby forever? At that age I was finding my own way about Rome, I was getting my own meals."

"We know all about that, darling. But we wouldn't want it to happen to our daughter, would we? We want her to have her childhood naturally——"

"Naturally!" Patrick exclaimed, and suddenly, as if he couldn't trust himself to speak again, turned on his heel and crossed the courtyard disappearing through an archway that no doubt led to his studio.

Lucie watched him go, smiling a little.

"Silly Daddy," she murmured, rumpling Juana's hair. "He does get cross, doesn't he? Come then, baby. Mummy promises to stay while you have your lesson."

Emily guessed that this would end in disaster. Either the child would refuse to concentrate or she would have great satisfaction in making a scene. Emily had an uneasy feeling that this was exactly what Lucie intended to happen. The piano lessons were to be a failure—so that there would be no reason for Emily to remain in the house. If she had been unwelcome last night she was doubly so this morning. Was that because she had attracted too much attention at dinner last night, or because of that foolish little accident in the maze? Surely Lucie didn't read anything into that! If so, she was as neurotically possessive of her husband as of her child.

But Juana looked rather sweet and comic perched on the music stool, her thin legs dangling. Her baby hands couldn't begin to span an octave. The first lessons would have to be very simple indeed.

Because of her own love for music Emily began her explanation of the keyboard with genuine enthusiasm. This child was too tense and sensitive not to have some talent. Who knew that it might not be for music?

"Goodness, how can she possibly understand that?" said Lucie, sprawled in a deep easy chair, smoking a cigarette in a long holder. "She's only just mastered her first reading books. All this C-D-E-F-G is only going to confuse her."

"If you wouldn't mind being quiet," Emily said politely. "Now, Juana, play these notes like I do."

"I can't," said Juana.

"Of course you can. Each finger like this."

"I can't. My fingers are too little. Mummy says they are."

"I don't think so. They're quite strong."

"They are too little. Mummy says so. Don't you, Mummy?" She swung round to appeal to her mother.

"Honey baby, Emily has asked me not to talk. She's the teacher. You pay attention to her."

"Why can't you talk? Why?"

Lucie shrugged eloquently. The pink deepened in Juana's cheeks.

"I really think," said Emily to Lucie, "that we'd get on better alone. You do distract her, you know."

"I hardly think there'll be a lesson at all without me here," said Lucie. "I've tried to warn you about my child's nervous system. You don't seem to understand any more than my husband does. But I admit you've hardly had time. Now come, Juana darling. Do what Emily says. Make a lovely sound."

"Why aren't you allowed to talk to me?" Juana demanded in a rising voice. "Aren't you ever going to be allowed to talk to me? Aren't you?"

"Of course I am, darling. But not during your lesson."

Juana flung herself off the stool.

"Then I won't have a lesson. Why must I? I hate lessons. My fingers are too little. Mummy! My fingers are too little." Having worked herself into that pitch of hysteria the child began to scream.

It was a repetition of the previous evening. Lucie held out her arms, and Juana flew into them to bury her head in her mother's breast and sob noisily. Lucie's dark eyes regarded Emily over her head.

"You see?" she said. "You say I shouldn't be here. You blame me for this. But without me I hate to think what would have happened."

Emily closed the lid of the piano. She was struggling to keep her temper. Where would they be if they all started screaming at one another?

"You don't begin to understand," said Lucie over the child's dying sobs, and there seemed to be a hint of desperation in her voice. "I can see that all you're going to say is that I don't know how to bring up a child. You simply don't try to realize her complexities."

Tell that to her father, Emily said silently. Or rather, don't tell him again, because he must be tired of hearing it.

She bit her lips and at last was able to say, quite calmly, "She's your child, you must do as you please," before she left the room.

Would she be invited to stay if she were not teaching Juana? Emily stood in her room in front of the open wardrobe regarding her clothes. Should she begin to pack? She had an impulse to fling everything into her cases because suddenly she hated this place. Everything was too loud and garish, the servants chattering in their endless shrill voices,

Juana screaming, the mid-day sun blindingly hot, the tumbling masses of flowers too bright, too outlandish. Everything was *extreme,* even that moment in the maze was too wildly exaggerated simply because Patrick's eyes had stopped resenting her, and his hands practically circling her waist had felt wonderfully supporting and strong.

But if her own emotions were going to fluctuate as extravagantly as Juana's, then she mustn't stay.

This time the knock on the door was perfectly audible. She crossed the room quickly to open it. Patterson, expressionless, but vaguely smug, as if she were pleased about something (Emily's failure with Juana?) stood there.

"The mistress wants to see you, miss."

"Now?"

"If you don't mind, miss. If it's inconvenient—"

Emily smoothed her hair. "I'll come at once. It's just that—"

"You're a bit put out," said Patterson. "So's the mistress. Mr. Fabrice went off to the shop without seeing her and that upset her. Then if there's one thing that drives her up the wall it's Miss Juana screaming."

"Where did you learn that expression, Patterson? Surely not in Spain."

"Good gracious, miss, because we live here it doesn't mean we're behind the times. I get letters from my young nephew who keeps me up to date."

"In England? Do you ever see him?"

"Not often, miss. But he'll be coming here on a visit one day soon. I'm looking forward to that. He wants to see the world. He's ever so ambitious. But come, miss. Don't keep the mistress waiting."

When Emily made to go along the corridor, she said, "No, downstairs, miss. She's about to go to the cemetery."

It was really Hannah the Governess this time. She sat very upright, very sombre, in black from head to foot. The large bouquet of carnations and roses that Emily had noticed earlier lay on the table beside her. So that was what they were for: Ferdie's grave.

"Well," she said abruptly, as Emily went up to her. "What went wrong? What was the cause of that unmannerly screeching?"

"I don't know, Cousin Hannah. You must ask your granddaughter."

"Come, come, you were there. Did you rap her knuckles? Not that it wouldn't have been justified."

The scene in the music room was too recent for Emily to be able to think of it dispassionately.

"I did nothing. Unfortunately, nothing at all. If I had managed to teach her a little it wouldn't have mattered so much. But in my opinion Juana is unteachable while her mother is with her. At least, I don't care to try again."

"Now, now, girl, don't you lose your temper, too. A good teacher remains calm always. I ought to know. Tomorrow you will try again."

"And if I refuse?"

Hannah cackled gently.

"You won't. You're too kind. It's written all over you. Dolly's kindness."

Emily sat on the stool beside Hannah.

"I don't see what that has to do with it."

"You don't? When in front of your eyes there's a child crying out for help, for understanding, for discipline—certainly for discipline, but more for love?"

"Love! I think she gets too much of that."

"Does she?" said Hannah, her eyes narrowed. She didn't elaborate that cryptic remark beyond adding, "Personally I find her very difficult to love, but you're young and tolerant and generous. You'll succeed better than me. I never was maternal, anyway. Yes, I think you'll try again tomorrow, and this time you'll have the child alone. I'll use a little discipline myself. I can, you know. My children still have a healthy respect for me."

"Cousin Hannah, Juana isn't interested in music. Besides, she's too young and undeveloped. It's a waste of time."

"Do you already know so well what she's interested in? I believe you've seen her twice, and each time she's had an attack of hysterics."

"I think she's frightened of something," Emily murmured, unwillingly feeling herself involved again. Ten minutes ago she had really washed her hands of that impossible child. But now— She had looked quaint and somehow pathetic perched on the music stool. If she were to look happy, really happy as a child should, she might be quite attractive. Even her father might be more tolerant towards her.

"Of course she's frightened of something," said Hannah. "A hundred things. What child isn't? I scare her to death myself. But I do care about that funny little green plant that must be taught to blossom. There's something under the hysterics. And the hysterics have got to stop. You can help, Emily. You're young, happy, uninvolved. You must help."

"What about her own mother?"

The old lady gave a small defeated shrug. "Lucie is thirty-two. Who can change her now? What she is, she is. Perhaps she's also frightened of something. She doesn't confide in me. I blame no one but myself for that. I wasn't good as a mother. I try to be better as a grandmother."

She put her dry cool old hand over Emily's.

"You wouldn't be the kind of person, Emily, who ran away from someone needing help."

For a moment Emily had the strangest feeling that the old lady was no longer talking about Juana, but about herself.

"So that's settled, isn't it? Tomorrow you try again."

"I can't teach Juana if she refuses to learn."

"Now, now, you're a clever girl, you can think up some ruse to take her attention. But I won't have that screeching. Remember! Now I must be off before the sun gets too hot. Every Thursday for the last ten years I've taken flowers to my dear husband's grave. That was, until my illness a few weeks ago. But if I can come downstairs to dinner, I have no reason for neglecting Ferdie any longer."

"And—my Aunt Dolly's grave?" Emily heard herself saying brashly.

"But, dear child, that isn't in Granada. That's in Madrid. Didn't your father tell you? Poor Dolly died there. I was trying to get her to the English hospital. The doctors in Granada were all Spanish. I didn't understand a word they said, nor they me. But oh, that nightmare journey. It never stopped raining, and I was coming down with typhus myself. I was shaking and shivering and trying to hold Dolly from falling. We'd got a train at last, and finally we even got to Madrid. But she died in the hospital there. By that time I was too ill to care. It was weeks before I was able to write details home—I doubt if I ever wrote them all. No, perhaps your father didn't know the whole story. It was so terribly painful. And, after all, nothing could be done. Dolly was gone—gone, poor pretty lamb. And she'd been so alive, nobody had been more alive. Ah well! Give me my stick, child."

"Wait a minute, Cousin Hannah. What about Dolly's lover? The man she had written she was going to marry. Was he terribly upset by her death?"

Cousin Hannah's eyelids fell the barest fraction.

"Oh, him. He'd disappeared long before. She'd had the sense to get rid of him."

"She had? I thought—Daddy said—it was you who got rid of him."

"Certainly I helped. Once I'd seen him. I frankly couldn't understand Dolly's infatuation for him. She was the flightiest creature, she fell in love with everyone. But she recovered just as quickly, fortunately. Oh, that was all over long before she died. I had married Ferdie by then. She'd been my bridesmaid."

"That must have pleased you," Emily couldn't help saying.

Hannah shot her a sharp glance.

"You think it gave me satisfaction to marry before Dolly, after all? Well, yes, it did. I'm only human and I'd been plain good old Hannah for long enough. It's no fun living in someone's shadow. She wanted to give me a complete trousseau but I didn't need much for the simple life Ferdie and I were going to lead. She did give me that old marriage chest that you might have noticed in your room, though. She'd bought it for herself, but when her love affair ended she didn't want it any more. Look at it when you go upstairs again. I thought you might like to use it yourself."

Emily never knew why that simple dry statement brought back all the excitement, the feeling of enchantment and expectation with which she had woken, but which the events of the morning had temporarily dispelled.

"I'm not planning to be married, Cousin Hannah."

"No? But who knows? You're pretty, you're in Spain, you have a marriage chest." Hannah's ugly face had a curious sad charm. "You'll be luckier than Dolly," she said.

Then Patrick came in. He helped Hannah to her feet, put her stick in her good hand, and said in a voice Emily hadn't heard him use before, a caressing velvet voice, "Now, darling, take your time. Ferdie will wait. He's in no hurry."

Hannah looked back at Emily.

"Patrick has taken me to Ferdie every week since he's been my son-in-law. How long is that now, Patrick?"

"Nine years. Mind the step now. You're doing fine."

"Patterson thinks I'm mad."

"She's probably right."

"Rash, perhaps. Not mad. Mad's a nasty word. And going to see Ferdie won't kill me. Emily didn't get on very well with Juana this morning."

"What did you expect?" said Patrick, looking at Emily with his appraising glance.

"I expect her not to be defeated by a child."

"She isn't fighting a child, Mamita."

"Oh, bosh, you mean Lucie! Really, Patrick, I don't know how you have so much patience with my wayward daughter. I suppose that's love. I suppose that's why Ferdie stood so much from me." She chuckled, a little breathlessly. She was finding the walk across the tiled floor and down the steps an ordeal. "I was no easy wife, either. But it avoids boredom in marriage, don't you agree?"

She paused a moment to lean on her stick.

"I have given Emily that old marriage chest of Dolly's. I thought it might amuse her."

Patrick turned to look back at Emily. Over Hannah's black-scarfed head their eyes met. It wasn't a physical touch this time. Yet Emily had the same moment of crazy heart-stopping excitement that she had had in the maze. What was more, she was certain that Patrick had it, too. His look of appraisal had gone. His eyes were very bright and intimate. For that moment in time they shared something. A thought, a feeling, an identity?

But for him it was quickly gone. It had to be. He said, "Good luck," in an easy teasing voice, and went off with Hannah, leaving her to prolong the impossible moment because she was not as practical as Patrick, and thought it did no harm to dream.

CHAPTER SIX

THE streets were almost empty when Emily, following Fabrice's directions, made her way to the little dark-windowed shop that was called, rather grandly, the Bowman Galleries.

It was siesta time. The shutters of the houses were closed, the shops shut. Men lounged in dark cool doorways, or women, who had no time to sleep, brought out a kitchen chair and sat in a patch of shadow sewing or making lace. A few cars passed. Donkey bells jingled as a docile trio of the little beasts followed their bare-footed owner. The sun lay like a hot blanket over the dust-coloured rooftops and the cobble-stones.

Fabrice opened the door to Emily's knock, and led her through the dark shop to his workroom at the back. It was a fascinating room, alive with the ticking of clocks. Every one of them went, Fabrice said. He never kept a clock, no matter how antique and beautiful, if it was beyond repair. It would be like a dead body, he said, its heart given out.

He was like a large bee in a very busy hive. But here he had an authority he didn't have at home. His plump hands moved very surely among the most delicate of the clocks: a French gilt travelling clock no more than an inch in diameter, a Dresden mantelpiece clock that was a whirl of fragile leaves and flowers, a Faberge shaped like an egg. His long heavy-jowled face was intent as he peered through the magnifying glass clamped in one eye and demonstrated to Emily how one small adjustment would restore the chimes to a beautiful little clock in a Sèvres porcelain case.

"I suppose I'm still a boy," he said, "but I'm fascinated with things that tick or whirr. Look at these musical boxes. I play them for Juana. That's her favourite." He pointed to one. "When it's wound a jack-in-the-box pops out. Oh, I see you've found the doll. That's supposed to be out of sight in case Juana comes in. It's for her birthday. It's an Edwardian clockwork doll. It curtseys when it's wound up. Maria's going to dress it in a new outfit. She's a good needle-woman. Most Spanish girls are. They haven't thrown away sewing boxes for typewriters yet."

Emily held the doll with its vaguely gruesome yellowed kid arms and legs, and its moon-like wax face.

"Will Juana like it?"

"When it's dressed, indeed she will. I admit it looks a little indecent now. I had to get rid of its clothes when I bought it. They were filthy. I'll touch up the face with a little paint. You'll be surprised. She'll be an elegant lady. And there's nothing at all wrong with her works. I'll show you."

Fabrice inserted a key into the doll's back and wound it gently. Then he balanced the creature squarely on its flat kid feet and, with a slight whirring and creaking, it performed a slow-motion curtsey.

But there was something macabre about those naked limbs like very old flesh, and the blank face. Emily gave the faintest shiver. She felt sure Juana would have hysterics at the sight of this thing that Fabrice handled so lovingly. She wanted to tell him to give it away or throw it away, but the pride in his face was too evident to be spoiled.

Perhaps he and Maria between them could perform a miracle and make it into a beautiful acceptable toy for a sensitive little girl. Anyway, it was a clever creature and Fabrice was very proud of it.

"When is Juana's birthday?"

"In a fortnight. I must smuggle this home tonight so Maria can begin work. It really doesn't seem nearly nine years since the day Patrick walked in and Lucie decided she was going to marry him."

"Just like that?"

"Love at first sight," Fabrice said seriously. "Mama wasn't at all pleased. She had wanted Lucie to marry a Spanish nobleman, no less. And Lucie was pretty then. Not so thin and edgy. But spoilt. She wanted the penniless English artist and that was that. She would have run off with him if Mama hadn't agreed at last?"

"And Patrick?"

"Oh, he was crazy about Lucie. So Mama gave them a grand wedding and ended up by falling in love with Patrick herself." Fabrice smiled tolerantly. "Lucie didn't take to being pregnant, though. She's vain. She hated not being able to wear smart clothes. Then Juana was born and she switched right round and adored the baby. Never let it out of her sight. Still doesn't, as you've noticed."

"Is it because— Do she and Patrick quarrel?"

"Always have. But they say reconciliations are half the fun in marriage. ı wouldn't know. All the same, they do seem to use that poor little wretch Juana as a pawn."

Interested as she was in Juana, Emily was suddenly thinking instead of the marriage chest in her bedroom. She had studied it carefully after Hannah had told her about it. The name of its first owner was carved into its side: "Isabella Herera, 1762." Isabella was gone long since, and so was Dolly, its most recent owner. But there was always a new bride, Emily thought. When the heavy carved lid was lifted the interior smelt of spices. The chest was empty and waiting for the hand-embroidered sheets and pillow cases and nightgowns of its next owner.

And Hannah was saying to Patrick, *How can you have so much patience with my wayward daughter, I suppose it's love* . . . and Patrick was looking at Emily, saying easily, airily, *Good luck.* . . .

The visit to the cemetery had been too much for Hannah. She had retired to her room and would not be leaving it again that day.

Juana, too, had been put to bed with a slight fever. A little sunstroke, perhaps, Lucie said, and blamed it on her escapade in the maze that morning.

"That useless maze," she said crossly. "Mama says Dolly kept the house because of it. She used to like her lovers to pursue her through it."

"Her lovers!" said Emily.

"Well, men, whoever they were. She wasn't the sort to be without men. Surely you can guess that from the way she looked."

Lucie's eyes swept over Emily and Emily knew she was thinking, not of Juana whose fair skin couldn't stand the hot sun, but of Patrick in the maze that morning. And that Emily didn't look the sort to be without men either.

"The servants use it now," she said.

"Use what?" Emily's mind was wandering.

"They make love in the maze. I hear them giggling from my room." Lucie's face was sharp with distaste. "I'll get rid of it one day. I'll put in another fountain and flowerbeds. Fabrice won't mind. The house will be mine and Fabrice's one day."

"Don't count your chickens, Miss Lucie."

Lucie turned sharply.

"Patterson!"

Patterson had known Lucie from the day she was born. If she observed perfect decorum with Hannah, she obviously let herself slip into a cosy familiarity with the rest of the family.

"Your mother's quite capable of leaving it to a refugee society, or anything, you know that well enough," said Patterson, not looking at Lucie but at Emily.

"Then you must stop her," said Lucie. "She'll do as you say."

"It's hardly my business, Miss Lucie."

"Oh, come off it, Patterson. Everything in this house is your business, and you know it. After all, it's your home, too. Fabrice and I won't be turning you out. But there's no knowing what a refugee might do." Lucie began to laugh, as if she had made a joke. "What nonsense you talk, Patterson. Never take any notice of her, Emily. She likes to pull our legs. The *Casa de Flor* a refugee home indeed! Mama isn't that mad."

Patterson shook her neat grey head and waddled to the door.

"There's no knowing how illness and old age can change a person. Going to the cemetery in the heat today! Would you call that sane? I wouldn't. But she won't listen to me in spite of what you think. What'll be the next thing she'll do?"

So Hannah's first sign of mental instability had been in sending for Emily, because she was harking back nostalgically to her girlhood. The next would be if she decided sentimentally to leave the *Casa de Flor*, which, after all, had been Dolly's, to Dolly's niece as a kind of poetic justice. There was no doubt Emily was Patterson's "refugee" and that this was the reason for Patterson's suppressed hostility. Her loyalty would naturally be towards Fabrice and Lucie, the children she had known since birth, and who would never turn her out.

But all this only existed in Patterson's head, Emily was sure. It was simply the insecurity of old age seizing her. Hannah was perfectly sane, a little deliberately eccentric perhaps, but certainly not mad.

Maria was in Emily's room when she went upstairs after breakfast the next morning. She started away from the mirror where she had been rolling her eyes in utter absorption. It was to make them larger, she told Emily with a complete lack of self-consciousness. So that her young man would think her pretty. Was she pretty? she wanted to know anxiously.

She was so gay and good-natured. Even if she were a servant all her life she would never be made into the repressed mould of poor old Patterson. What did it do to a woman's soul to say obediently, "Yes, madam. No, madam," all her life? Emily wondered why the thought of Patter-

son oppressed her, and turned gladly to this happy unin-
hibited creature.

"I think you're very pretty. Doesn't your young man think
so?"

Maria giggled. "My mother says, never believe what a
man tells you until he has the wedding ring on your finger."

"I expect she's right. Do any girls in Spain not get
married?"

Maria looked shocked.

"But never, senorita. Unless they're crippled or something
terrible. What else is there for a woman?"

"And are they always happy?" Emily persisted.

"Certainly. They have babies. They love their husband.
There might be things, a bad mother-in-law, sometimes a
cruel husband. But they're not unhappy for no reason. Not
like—"

Maria stopped suddenly, and with a strange little jump of
her heart Emily knew what she had been going to say. Not
like Patrick and Lucie. . . .

"I shall have six children," said Maria, turning to toss
the sheets vigorously off the bed. "Not just one. One is too
alone. She has to have dolls instead of brothers and sisters."

"You mean Juana?"

"*Si*, senorita." Maria's face sparkled. "I have this doll to
make beautiful for her birthday. I have a—what do you call
it?—fashion to follow. Petticoats, skirts, a real hat. But it
isn't the same as a baby sister or brother. Is it, senorita?"

And that was a question that made Emily wonder if Lucie
had refused to have more children. Fabrice had said she
had hated being pregnant. Patrick, she knew, with certainty,
would like a son. And not a weakling child like Juana. She
began to imagine Patrick's son, strong, blue-eyed. . . .

"The *nina* has too many bad dreams," Maria went on.
"It is sad."

"About this imaginary old woman?"

"Imaginary?" Maria frowned, her excellent English suddenly failing her.

"Someone who isn't there. I'm told that house is empty."

"Ah! Ah! You mean La Loca, senorita."

"But isn't the house empty?"

"Pilar and Pablo live there. They keep the house for its
owner who never comes. But never. They say he lives in
Madrid, but no one really knows. Pilar and Pablo are old
and queer and unfriendly. They never talk to people. It

isn't natural." Maria rolled her eyes, looking affronted. Everyone in Spain talked.

"Then Pilar is the one Juana has seen. The one called La Loca."

Maria had finished straightening the bed and was now busily dusting.

"They do say this nobleman, this Count, has his wife locked up there. Because she is mad. *Loca,* you understand? At least that's the story. I do not listen." Maria shook her head vigorously.

"But I thought that was something that had happened long ago. A legend."

"Not long ago, senorita. So they say. But no one talks. Pablo doesn't hear. Deaf as a stone, is that what you say? And his wife never goes out to market. Sometimes to church, but she doesn't talk to people. It is strange."

Maria refused to be mystified for long. She began to laugh, saying, "Here I am telling you marriage in this country is happy, and now I say a poor wife is locked up. But she must have been very bad. Or perhaps she was always mad, and there was to be no—"

Maria groped for the word, and Emily finished, "Scandal?"

"Ah, yes. Spanish men do not like scandal." Maria nodded emphatically, approving of this. She giggled. "Perhaps the senorita will find out for herself."

Juana was sitting up in bed cutting out paper dolls while her mother watched fondly. Emily had tapped at the door and been bidden to come in.

"Is she still ill?" she asked in concern.

"No, she's quite better. Aren't you, pet? But we're having a quiet day."

"No lesson?" Emily asked.

Lucie frowned. "Oh, yes, she's to have that. But a very short one. I'll send her to you in an hour. Will that be all right?" Lucie was being very formal. Emily wondered what pressure Hannah had brought to bear on her daughter. Probably the threat that if Juana were not to learn anything at home she would take Patrick's side and have the child sent to school.

"I shall go only if I please," Juana said in a prim voice.

"Of course, darling. But remember what I promised. Dinner downstairs and you can stay up late."

"And Daddy won't be cross?"

"I won't let him be cross. What an idea! Do you think Mummy can't manage that?"

It wasn't to be supposed that Lucie, defeated over the music lessons, wouldn't get her own way back in some other way. She was very foolish. There was attractiveness in her thin, austere face. Her enormous black eyes were beautiful. Yet somehow she had a way of making one feel she was as lost inside as Juana was.

Who wasn't lost at some time in his life? Waiting for Juana to come down, Emily sat at the piano and let her own lostness sweep over her as she began to play. But it was no good. She couldn't have thought a miracle would have happened and that her finger would respond again. The lovely harmonies of the Mozart concerto stumbled, were marred. This vital part of her life was gone. For the first time since the accident had happened something unknotted, dissolved, inside her and the tears ran down her cheeks. She crashed her hands in discord on the piano keys, and wept.

"Oh, come," said Patrick's voice from the other end of the room. "Don't do that."

Emily gasped. The shock stopped her tears.

She swung around on the stool to see him crossing the room. He must have been sitting in the shadow near the window and she hadn't noticed him.

"I don't cry," she said defensively. "I'm not a crier."

"You'd have a good reason."

"I suppose so." She wiped away the dampness on her cheeks with the back of her hand. She hadn't expected that sort of tenderness in his eyes. She had seen him angry, and aloof, and hard, and yesterday, for a moment, he had been a man looking at a woman with quick intimate interest. But this tender concern was another thing. It touched something too vulnerable in herself. She could only combat it with flippancy.

"It was only because I made such a ghastly noise. As my music master used to say, 'How can you be sure Mozart isn't listening?' "

"It sounded fine to me, even with a bad finger."

"Not to me. I didn't know you were listening."

"You wouldn't have played if you had known I was?"

Emily nodded. "That's true. After all, you don't show me your pictures."

He looked surprised. And pleased, she thought. "Do you want to see them? Are you interested?"

"Of course I'm interested. What do you think? That I'm deaf and blind to everything but music?"

"Then come over to my studio when you're finished with Juana. You are giving her a lesson?"

"Yes, in a few minutes."

"That's good. Don't stand any nonsense from her. Make her behave."

And now he looked as usual, his eyes aloof, a little hard, and quite unreadable. He was Juana's father again, and Lucie's husband.

It was unreasonable of her to think that for a few minutes he had been neither of those things. It was not only unreasonable but dangerous to begin toying with those sort of thoughts. At least she could control her mind, even if her body kept remembering, with a shiver of delight, the feel of his hands. That had been yesterday, and accidental at that. Oh, lord, she couldn't be falling in love with Lucie's husband. That really would be something to cry about.

She had an idea about Juana, though. She was suddenly feeling extraordinarily alive and inspired.

Juana liked dolls. She quickly made a doll out of her handkerchief, knotting a miniature head, and tiny fists. She set it on the end of the keyboard, and when Juana came in, pushed through the door by Maria, she said to the reluctant and apprehensive child, "We have an audience, see? She's waiting to hear you play."

It turned out that Juana had a smile of astonishing sweetness and delight. Her plain waxen little face was quite transformed by it.

"I've never seen a handkerchief doll before. Is she for me?"

"Yes. But she lives in the piano. She only comes out during lesson time. She's a doll who's crazy about music, especially about five-finger exercises."

"Five-finger exercises?" said Juana, wriggling on to the stool.

"Like this." Emily began to play slowly, making the small fingers follow her.

She hardly dared to believe that the child grew genuinely absorbed. When finally she wearied of painstakingly picking out the notes she looked up at Emily with a look of triumph and pleasure that gave her a sudden heart-stopping likeness to her father.

"Can I play now? As good as you?"

"Shall I show you how you'll play one day?"

All the time that Emily was telling herself to be cautious, not to test her intuition that here was a child of talent and sensitivity, not to find out things that would draw her to the pathetic little creature and involve her too deeply and painfully with this family, her impulsiveness was driving her on. Just as she knew she would deliberately seek Patrick's company, she also knew she must help Juana over her fears and apprehensions.

It was no use to fight her own nature which was involvement, not standing aside, too quick emotions. She supposed it was true that she was like Dolly, reckless, impulsive, heading blindly towards being hurt. Somehow she knew now that Dolly had been bitterly, grievously hurt.

She played the Brahms lullaby for her small audience, the tow-haired child and the handkerchief doll. When she stopped Juana said only in her imperious voice, "Again!" And after the second time she wanted to be shown how to play it herself. She listened with attention while Emily explained how long it would be before she could attempt such a thing. She looked about to have one of her fits of tantrums (which Emily was sure that Lucie, within earshot, was eagerly awaiting), but suddenly she changed her mind and gave an unexpectedly adult shrug.

"I suppose I'll have to grow up, like Daddy says. It's an awful bore. Can I go now? Mummy gets lonely without me."

"Yes, you can go now."

"Can I take the handkerchief doll?"

"No, I told you, she lives in the piano."

"But Mummy wants to see her." Again there was the trembling on the edge of hysteria. Emily met the wide pale blue eyes steadily. With her pale eyelashes and pale skin the child was like an unfledged chicken. But somehow appealing.

"Won't you play for me again if I take her?"

"No, I don't suppose I will."

"Will you get La Loca to come for me?"

Emily was shocked. "Whatever makes you say that?"

"Maria says that. So does Concita. But I'm not frightened. Truly I'm not. I'll go and throw stones at her old window.

And then I'll run as fast as I can before she looks out." Juana paused rather breathlessly, obviously appalled by her daring. "Can I go to Mummy now?"

"Yes, I told you you could. And Juana. Listen, honey. There isn't any old woman there. There isn't a La Loca."

"But I've seen her," said the child simply. "She is there."

CHAPTER SEVEN

EMILY forgot about the imaginary La Loca the moment she entered Patrick's studio. She remembered that he had told her to wear yellow. He seemed to have an obsession with that color. For almost all the canvases hung or propped against the walls were in tones of ochre, orange, a reddish color like smouldering flames, and the clearest pale yellow, the afterglow of sunset. It was like a sunburst, full of warmth, vitality, excitement.

She stood staring in absorption. Patrick emerged from behind his easel and watched her. She looked from a Spanish village washed with early sunlight to a stretch of dry burnt red hillside pitted with the shadows of olive trees beneath a flaring sky, a field of maze ripened to a rich gold, the seamed sun-blackened face of a peasant with his mules.

"But this country isn't yellow," she murmured. "It's dusty white, it's the colour of bones, or cinnamon, or smoky green."

"It's blazing with sun," said Patrick. "Whether you see it or not with your naked eye, it's always there, that dazzling yellow. It's in your subconsciousness. You never forget it, even at midnight."

"It's magnificent," said Emily. "And yet it's a torment!"

"Yes. It's a torment."

"I see it in the eyes of this old man. Yet he'd never live anywhere else. His face says that. Is that what you feel, too?"

"That I'd never live anywhere else? Perhaps. Painting dogs in England never appealed to me very much."

"Will these sell?"

"I hope so. Some of them, anyway. I'm getting ready for an exhibition in Madrid."

"Will they sell well?"

"Reasonably well. Enough for me, at least."

She had said the wrong thing. The look of pure enthusiasm and satisfaction in his face had gone. She had made him think of money, and the necessity for it if one had an expensive wife. Lucie sat in here often. Where did she sit, with her poised dark head, her sullen face, among this flaring color?

"Do you want figures?" Patrick said. "I shall hope to average about three hundred pounds a picture. That, of course, is only a tenth of what Hannah would make on the sale of a Goya, supposing she had a Goya for sale. And she has had."

"She doesn't tell you you would be better occupied hunting for art treasures!" Emily exclaimed.

"Hannah's a realistic woman. We came to an arrangement long ago. I work half the time for myself, half for her. Now she's ill, of course, it isn't going to be so simple. If we're to keep up the standards of the *Casa de Flor*—"

"You and Fabrice, too!" said Emily. "Who wants these standards? Only Hannah?"

"And what's it to do with you, Emily?" came Lucie's cool voice from the doorway. "Are you taking on the household accounts as well as the education of my daughter?"

Emily hadn't been standing near Patrick, not even within arm's reach. Yet Lucie's eyes made her feel instantly guilty. The guilt must be in her own mind. She had wanted to be standing close to Patrick. And Lucie had expected it. Didn't she trust her husband?

All this raced through her mind, while Patrick, with the frown scored between his brows again, said sharply, "Where's Juana?"

"With Maria. Is that wrong? You're always telling me not to have her with me so much."

"Of course it's not wrong. Come and sit down if you're staying."

Lucie made a little grimace.

"That doesn't sound exactly welcoming. Have I interrupted something?"

"I was showing Emily my work."

"And explaining financial returns? Let's hope there are some. Did you tell Emily how much we need them?"

Patrick ran his fingers through his hair with a controlled movement.

"Forget it. All this talk about money gets to be a bore." He stabbed his finger at the painting of the peasant. "I could live on what I'll get for that for a year. That makes life simple. But with the frills—"

"Which you enjoy," said Lucie. She went to tuck her arm into Patrick's, pressing her cheek against his sleeve. "Would you like to see me dressed like a peasant? Or Juana barefoot? And you do have rather a weakness for French wine. Spanish would be much cheaper. But of course money's a bore. I wish we didn't have to talk about it. And Emily," she went on, looking sideways at Emily, "hasn't said a word. Don't tell me—she thinks your work stupendous."

"I do," said Emily. She refused to say more although Lucie was expecting her to, waiting for the excuse for her jealousy to flare afresh. "Juana was very good at her lesson," she added. "I think she may have a talent for music."

"How can you possibly tell?" Lucie's eyes flashed stormily. "A mere baby playing a five-finger exercise."

"I agree," Emily said calmly. "It's much too early to know whether she will be a musician herself. But she'll have appreciation. She's very intelligent, you know."

"You sound surprised," Lucie exclaimed. "Did you think my child a half-wit?"

"Who could blame her if she did?" said Patrick. "The way the little devil screeches." He gave Lucie a small push. "If you're staying, sit down and be quiet. I want to work."

"I'll stay a little while," said Lucie, as if she were conferring a favour. "Emily, Mama wants to see you. She says she's scarcely set eyes on you since you arrived. I told her you seemed to be in great demand. Fabrice, Patrick, Juana. But Juana's a good thing, at least, because now I'll really get more time with my husband. Won't I, darling?"

Emily went before Patrick answered, or Lucie turned her great brilliant eyes from him. Half-way down the stairs she found she had left her handbag and automatically ran back up the stairs to get it. But at the door of the studio she hesitated as Lucie's voice, half angry, half sobbing, came very clearly, "Patrick, she's stealing my baby already! It's true she is! I'm shut out of the music room, and Juana doesn't even have time to look at me when she comes out.

All she can say is something about a doll Emily gave her. That's no way to teach a child, by bribing her."

"But there were no hysterics," Patrick pointed out.

"Oh, I suppose you think that in one hour this paragon has cured her while I've never been able to. No, don't say anything." Lucie was getting near hysteria herself. "I can see you'd only defend Emily. It's her hair, I suppose. Why are men so besotted with blondes?"

"I once liked black hair," Patrick said.

"Once!"

"Why do you tear yourself to pieces like this?" His voice was low and full of pity.

Emily turned and went quietly downstairs. It didn't matter about her bag. She knew those two were in each other's arms. It was all very well to puzzle over and criticise Lucie for her stupidity and strange jealousy. But she wasn't sure how she would behave herself if she were to see them in each other's arms. It was an experience better avoided.

It was unfortunately her day for overhearing things. Hannah's bedroom door stood wide open, and Patterson's voice came clearly, even before Emily was half-way along the passage.

"I wouldn't want to have to take her on a visit, madam."

Hannah's voice sounded tired. "That won't be necessary, Patterson. As you very well know."

"I'm glad to hear it, madam. Now, madam, you've hardly touched your beef tea. And it's so nourishing. Just what you need."

"It's kind of you to be so solicitous of my welfare, Patterson. After fifty years. Quite a triumph."

"Don't be silly, madam." Patterson's voice was brusque. "Where would I be without you? Now will you take a nap, and I'll send Miss Doll—I beg your pardon, madam, Miss Emily, away."

"Don't boss me so much, Patterson. I've scarcely said two words to Emily yet. Go away and leave us alone."

(A visit . . . Where? And who might have to be taken? Emily?)

She tapped on the door, and Hannah's voice, strong now, asked her to come in. Hannah, a small ivory figure, with her hair piled grandly on top of her head, a lacy wrap round her shoulders, and rings on her fingers, was propped up against silk-covered pillows. Patterson picked up a tray and left the room, but not without a sideways warning glance at Emily. Don't stay long, the glance said. Patterson was indeed solicitous of her mistress's well-being.

"Come and sit down, close to me," Hannah said. "I was just saying to Patterson that we've scarcely exchanged two words, yet. It was a mistake going to the cemetery yesterday. I was exhausted afterwards. But I like to look after my dead. What are you looking at?"

"This room. It's beautiful. So many lovely things."

"Ah!" Hannah's eyes glinted with pleasure. "You like beautiful things? You know something about them?"

"Not very much. Daddy taught me a little, particularly when he knew I was coming here. We spent days in the Victoria and Albert museum."

"Now that's interesting. Perhaps we can employ you better than in giving music lessons to a spoilt child. By the way, I hear you managed very well this morning."

"Juana was very sweet."

"I'm glad to hear it. It proves that she needs to be less with her mother. Too much loving is as bad as too much hating. Both ways someone gets destroyed. You're too young to know that."

But she was beginning to find out. She had seen Lucie with Patrick. Was that love or hate?

"Yes, that's a beautiful clock," Hannah's voice came, as Emily studied the delicate edifice. "I've refused again and again to sell it. But I'm afraid the day is coming. One day I'll lie here in my bed in a bare room."

"Everyone in this house talks the same way," Emily burst out. "Yet here you are surrounded with very valuable things."

"It's our shop window," Hannah said tiredly. "When we sell that we're finished. In the meantime we have debts. And after all mine and Ferdie's work. It seems unfair. If I hadn't had this illness, if Fabrice were the son I wanted, if old age didn't stab one in the back . . . and of course I have spoilt my children, accustomed them to nothing but the best, and now they refuse to change. Lucie still expects to shop at a couturier in Madrid or Paris, and Patrick, bless him, struggles to give her what she wants. He should never have been saddled with an expensive wife, but at that time none of us thought of this day."

"Surely he'd have married her, anyway. Wasn't he in love?"

"In love? A young man is always in love. Oh, yes, Lucie

was a fascinating creature. But I should have known better. It was another of my mistakes."

"I'm sure you haven't made many mistakes."

Hannah smiled, patted Emily's hand.

"Bless you, dear. And you're quite right. I haven't made many mistakes. Perhaps that's why the ones I did make were so disastrous. But that's all over," she said briskly. "Presently I'm going to get up. Do look out of the window at my view. Isn't it superb? I lie here and listen to the bells. Dolly told me old Aunt Isabella bought the *Casa de Flor* for the maze and for this view. And now I am the one who enjoys it. Does that seem wrong to you?"

"No. Not if Dolly left it to you. She must have wanted you to enjoy it."

Hannah sighed, settling into her pillows.

"Yes, that's commonsense. I have the house, and this ring that never leaves my finger," she held out her hand to display the huge aquamarine that was out of proportion to her thin finger, "and a nightgown she gave me for my wedding night. I've always kept that. That's all that's left of Dolly. Except for you, of course."

"What about me?" That faintest uneasiness touched her again.

"You're wondering why I asked you here? It certainly wasn't just to discipline my granddaughter. It was simply because I hoped we might have a little love for each other. Is that so foolish?"

Emily was deeply touched. She had never expected humility from this proud old woman. Nor this admission of loneliness.

"It isn't foolish at all," she said warmly. She watched the topaz eyes that were scarcely concealing their anxiety. "Nor impossible. I love you already."

Hannah's lips trembled violently. But her voice came out steadily and triumphantly, "And that old fool Patterson said I was a crazy old woman."

"She's jealous of her preserves. It's natural, after being with you for so long. She loves you, too."

Hannah gave a short, dry laugh.

"I doubt the old devil knows the meaning of the word. Dolly used to think that she loved her, but that was long ago. And one thing I don't like is to be called crazy. It hurts." She reflected sombrely. "One can't help being afraid it might be true."

Then she briskly dismissed her sentimental mood.

"But I didn't send for you to talk about myself. I want you to talk to me. Tell me about your home, your childhood, how you became such a good pianist, if you've been in love. Come now. This is what I've been waiting to hear."

After Emily had gone the room seemed not quite so light. Which was sheer imagination, in this brilliant unchanging light with scarcely ever a cloud over the sun.

Hannah had listened with absorbed interest to the story of the simple uncomplicated childhood with two loving parents, one of them Dolly's brother, with more than a touch of Dolly's wildness and extravagance and generosity. Then to the musical ambitions and the years of practice and dedication that had led to such tragically short-lived success. Why, the child hadn't even had time to fall in love. Now, with her career so abruptly taken from her, she was dangerously ready. She would fall into the arms of the first attractive man she met. So one must be careful. She mustn't be allowed to suffer Dolly's tragedy. But the discipline of her career had repressed any wildness or unpredictability she might have inherited from her father or Dolly. She was intelligent, warm-hearted and responsive. What a wife she was going to make some man.

Hannah stirred in frustration. If only she hadn't contracted this abominable illness she would have had the greatest pleasure in taking Emily to Madrid and Seville to show her off, doing things in the style in which she had done them for Lucie. Not that Lucie had taken full advantage of her opportunities when she had fallen in love with a penniless artist. But Patrick had a way of breaking down one's defences. And he was going to do well, if Lucie didn't stop him.

But Emily was another matter. Someone else would have to take her to Madrid. She must visit the Prado. She must see the mosque at Cordoba, and that age-bleached fantastic old city of Toledo. If only . . . Hannah struggled up, her face tightened with the effort of moving her stiffened body. She *would* overcome this illness.

She lifted the little silver bell by her bed and rang it vigorously. When Patterson came, she said peremptorily, "I shall go down to lunch. Help me dress."

"Is that wise, madam? Wouldn't you rest quietly here and go down to dinner tonight?"

"I shall do both. Don't bully me, Patterson. I'm still alive, and I shall stay that way for a long time."

"I'm glad to hear it, madam."

"I have something to live for now. That makes all the difference."

"A linen suit, madam? The white or the beige?"

"I even believe Emily may learn a little of the business. She's intelligent and observant. I must talk to Fabrice and Patrick. She might find it interesting to go to one of the important sales. I suppose that dreary beige, Patterson. But I'll dress it up with my combs and my ear-rings and my fan. Oh, and Patterson—"

Patterson turned, waiting.

"I've made up my mind at last about my beloved Louis the Fifteenth clock. Fabrice says he has a buyer. I'll let him sell it. Even though it breaks my heart. Ferdie bought it for me on our silver wedding anniversary."

"I remember, madam."

"Don't look so bored, Patterson. I realize you have no sympathy for the minutes and hours ticked away for lovers. I can see you think I'm in my second childhood. You've thought that ever since my illness."

"You were never one for being sentimental, madam. You must admit that."

She was standing with the letter she had snatched from Dolly in her hand.

"*How could you?*" she cried. "*How could you have so little pride?*"

Dolly was sitting very straight, her face white except for patches of red on her cheekbones.

"*But, Hannah! I've been so crushed and cowardly. I suddenly remembered Papa saying, 'Always fight for your rights.' So shouldn't I fight for my happiness?*"

"*So you think happiness is your right? You, Dolly Bowman, have some special dispensation for it! The sun must shine on you, if no one else!*"

Dolly leaned away from Hannah.

"*You're saying that as if you hate me.*"

"*Don't be such a little idiot. I'm only telling you to have more backbone. You face the first rebuff in your life and you go to pieces. Oh, Dolly! How could you pursue a man!*"

"*I was only writing—*" *Dolly faltered. "It seemed such a good idea.*"

"*And if he did come, after all this time, what would he*

think of you? Have you looked at yourself in the mirror lately?"

"I know I look washed out. It's so hot. At first I liked the heat, but this summer it drains me." She began to laugh unsteadily, "And it's you who's having the baby, not me."

Hannah looked down at her pityingly.

"Shall I tear this up?"

"I—I suppose so." Dolly's face was still, submissive, without light.

"If he comes, he must come of his own free will," Hannah said. "You can't have taken leave of your senses so much as not to know that. I think you sit in the sun too much. It addles your brain."

Hannah came back shudderingly to the present, the big sunny bedroom and Patterson's ever watchful figure. She wouldn't be surprised if Patterson had some extra antennae that heard those voices in her head, and saw Dolly in all those lost guises.

"Yes, no one ever thought I was sentimental," she said drily. "No one gave me credit for wanting happiness like other people. Well, never mind. The clock shall go. I suppose the money will be pleasant."

She regarded Patterson beneath her heavy eyelids.

Patterson said, with her well-trained lack of expression, "Money is always pleasant."

CHAPTER EIGHT

EMILY hadn't told anyone where she was going. With a map of the city she was able, quite easily, to find her way to the Albaicin. It wasn't more than a half mile walk from the *Casa de Flor*. It was a matter of minutes, then, to find the Calle de Fatima, the street in which La Loca was reputed to live.

Nor was it hard to identify the house, for there was only one among the old grey mansions that had an overgrown garden, with morning glory tumbling over the rusted gates. It looked quite deserted. The paint had peeled off the walls, the closed shutters were faded to a drab olive. One hung open, as if its hinge had broken, but the window it disclosed was dark and empty. There were none of the colorful rioting plants in pots that the Spaniards so loved on the balconies. The poor old house looked as if it had been neglected and unloved for years.

Even if it were owned by a rich aristocrat who lived abroad, one would have thought he would have either sold it, or had some care for it. Perhaps he was a miser who wouldn't pay the caretakers sufficient money, or else the caretakers were dishonest and counted on his never appearing to check on their stewardship. Perhaps he was an eccentric or an invalid.

In the blinding sun there was certainly an air of melancholy about this strange deserted place. A stray white cat, as thin as a shadow, appeared in the gateway, but clawed at Emily when she attempted to touch it. A hostile ghost, it disappeared into the undergrowth.

There was, Emily noticed, a stone gargoyle beneath each window, ugly leering objects that may well have been what frightened Juana and led her to having fantasies about the house. She could understand the eerie attraction that lured the child here.

But it was uncomfortable. One could almost shiver, in spite of the hot sun. Emily found herself wanting to get away as quickly as possible. She had come during siesta time so that the streets would be empty. But as she turned to go she saw a woman watching her from a distance away. Or had she merely mistaken her way, for as Emily began to walk towards her, she turned and went down a side street? She was a short stout woman dressed in a dark brown dress and with a scarf tied round her head. She was the shape of a million elderly Spanish women who had grown fat on oily food, wine, and child-bearing. It was odd that she had such a resemblance to Patterson. Patterson didn't look remotely Spanish in her spotless white cap and apron.

But how would she look in a dark brown dress with a scarf round her head? As anonymous as any Spanish peasant?

When Emily reached the side street the woman had disappeared, so there was no way of knowing who she had been. Anyway, it was unimportant. Except that if it had been Patterson, why had she wanted to avoid being seen?

When she got back to the *Casa de Flor,* Patterson, in her dazzlingly starched white cap and apron, was talking to the Englishman, Mr. Digby Field, in the cool tiled hall. She showed no sign of having been out in the sun. Her cheeks had their usual look of pink and white well-being, her eyes, flicking a glance towards Emily, were as cool as pebbles under water.

"You'll have to wait, sir. I never disturb the mistress during siesta, especially since her illness."

"Quite. I should have known better than to call at this time." Digby Field turned to Emily. "But I see everyone isn't afraid of the afternoon sun. Where have you been?"

Emily pushed back the hair from her hot forehead.

"Exploring. I seem to have too much energy. I must have a cold drink. Will you have one, too?"

"You'll have to get it yourself," said Patterson. "There'll be no one in the kitchen."

"Haven't you picked up the local customs yourself, Patterson?" Emily asked lightly. "Don't you have a siesta?"

"I came down to answer the door, miss," Patterson answered primly. Her shoes clacked as she walked across the tiled floor. Emily, about to go to the kitchen to make cool drinks, hesitated, something puzzling her.

"I won't stay for a drink, thank you," Digby Field was saying. "I'm catching the afternoon plane to Madrid. I just wondered if your cousin, Mrs. Romero, knows about this sale at the *Palacio del Sol* outside Toledo next week.

"Does she?" he repeated when Emily didn't answer.

"Does she what? I'm sorry, I didn't catch what you said."

"You were listening to something else."

Yes, she had been. Patterson's footsteps. And she knew now what was wrong. Patterson usually wore soft-soled shoes in the house. She was now wearing her street shoes.

"Perhaps you'd give her this catalogue. And tell her if she can find me an eighteenth-century tapestry I'll be interested. That's all I called for, so I'll be off."

Patterson didn't need to wake Hannah, for she was awake and up. She was sitting at the painted Italian chest of drawers. She had opened the bottom drawer and rummaged about in a muddle of garments to find at last the thin lawn nightdress with its modest neckline and sleeves edged with handmade lace. Hannah was surprised that its pristine whiteness had yellowed. It had been wrapped up and out of the light for so long.

Dolly had meant the gift kindly. She hadn't even reminded Hannah that it had been meant to be her own wedding nightgown. Only her huge sorrowful eyes had said that. Hannah would have much preferred not to wear it at all, but when she compared it with her own threadbare unadorned ones, she had known a bridegroom deserved better. Her marriage might be practical and unromantic, but it was for life, and it ought to be given some sort of chance. So she had brushed her hair, silky and long, but thin and straight as a poker, pinched her cheeks to make them red, and put on Dolly's nightgown. . . .

"Whatever are you doing, madam?" Patterson exclaimed.

"Living in the past, Patterson. An unhealthy occupation. Is it teatime already?"

"It's only just past four. That Mr. Field's downstairs. He's talking about a sale you should go to. Not if I know it, I said to myself."

"What sale, Patterson?" Hannah asked indifferently. She was tired. She hadn't slept, and she was still thinking of Dolly.

"I only heard as I was leaving the room, madam. At the *Palacio del Sol.*"

Hannah drew in her breath with a hiss.

When she did speak she said testily, "Why does Digby Field think he can tell me how to run my business? At Toledo," she added. "How could I get there?"

"You couldn't, madam, and that's flat."

Hannah said very slowly, wondering why it was sadness, not relief, that she felt. "Then he's dead, Patterson."

"Must be, madam."

"I wonder what happens to his estate. Why are you looking at me like that, Patterson?"

"You look ill, madam. I'll help you back to bed."

Hannah snapped her fingers irritably. "No, no, no. I don't need rest. I need to think. I remember there was a painting Don Jaime thought might have been a Rembrandt. I'd like to see that." She remembered Don Jaime's distant haughty voice speaking in impeccable English, "My family is very old, Miss Bowman. One of my ancestors was ambassador to England at the time Philip married your Queen Mary. An unbalanced woman."

"A very unbalanced woman," she had said evenly.

"You're scarcely thinking of going to that sale, madam?" Patterson was exclaiming.

Hannah got to her feet, staggered, and reached angrily for her stick.

"Oh, the devil take my old bones! Why does this happen now when I'm a cripple? Why couldn't it have happened ten years ago when Ferdie was alive?"

"Well, don't take on, madam. You have to give up one day. You can't get the light of battle in your eye at the news of every interesting sale in the country. That's all past for you."

"Hold your tongue, Patterson! Do I need to be reminded every minute of the day? Helplessness, dependence. How I loathe it!"

Patterson advanced, holding out her stout arm.

"Don't take on so, madam. You have me to help you."

"I know, Patterson." Hannah grudgingly took the offered arm. "But how can we know you won't be taken first? You're getting very short of breath. I hear you on the stairs." Hannah cackled at her macabre joke, then sat down again, breathing heavily herself. "Let me rest a minute. Then I'll go down and see Mr. Digby Field. I wonder what he has his eye on at Toledo. If it's a good enough commission—" Her excitement was growing again. She lowered her eyelids so as not to let Patterson see it. She was determined not to be defeated. She had a most avid desire to see the *Palacio del Sol*. She always had had. And now Don Jaime was dead and she didn't need to fear seeing his hawk face again, she could go untroubled. Uninvited, too. It was a delicious irony. She had another inspiration. She would take Emily. The girl could look after her, and in addition have her first lesson in the selecting and buying of antiques. But most of all it would make the irony more exquisite.

Life came full circle. Oh, she was far, far from being dead.

"I don't know what you're planning, madam, but I can guess it's some mischief."

Hannah looked impatiently at Patterson's stolid face. Bother the woman. That would be another battle to fight. But she was still the mistress. If she made up her mind to go to Toledo, that was entirely her own business.

"I'm thinking of that picture. If it were a Rembrandt—"

"Begging your pardon for mentioning it, madam, but where would you get the kind of money to bid for a Rembrandt?"

"Oh, don't be so stupid, Patterson! I would be bidding for

something by a much lesser artist. A few hundred—"

"That's money, too," Patterson observed.

Hannah was angry. "Mind your own business! If this came off, it would solve all our difficulties. I haven't had my last gamble yet."

Life was flaming in her. She hadn't felt so well for a long time.

She would take Emily to Toledo. She would have one more triumph.

"Help me to dress, Patterson. I'll go down to Mr. Field now."

"If that's as far as you're going, madam. You wouldn't be so mad as to let him persuade you to go to that sale?"

"I wish you wouldn't keep on using that word, Patterson," Hannah said wearily. "I'm as sane as I've ever been."

"Well—there's no fool like an old fool," Patterson said irritatingly. "And another thing, madam. You'll have to find more to occupy your young cousin from England."

Hannah's eyelids flicked up.

"Oh?"

Patterson was straightening clothes in the wardrobe. She deliberately kept Hannah waiting for her explanation.

At last she said, "She's too inquisitive. Always asking questions."

"Naturally. She wants to get to know us."

"Hasn't learnt to keep out of the hot sun, either. Wanders about the streets at all hours."

There was a long silence. Then Hannah said, "She'll soon have seen everything. She'll settle down."

"How long were you planning her visit to be, madam?"

"Why, Patterson? Is she worrying you?"

"No, madam."

"Then that's a good thing, because I don't mean to part with Emily for a long time." Hannah's eyes were half closed, hiding their tenderness. "Probably not at all."

She was only amused at Patterson's explosive breath.

"Well, I declare. I never thought you'd get so soft in your old age."

"That's better than being a busybody. You must watch that, Patterson. It's a familiar temptation for old maids."

CHAPTER NINE

THE thing one had to admire about Hannah was her ideas of grandeur.

This hotel suite, for instance. There were two bedrooms, two bathrooms, and a sitting-room. Hannah was at present asleep (one hoped) in one of the bedrooms, while Emily, unable to stay late in bed on this heavenly Madrid morning, had thrown her shutters open long since and contemplated the shining clarity of the day.

Poverty was obviously the last thing Hannah understood. Either all that talk of imminent bankruptcy was wildly exaggerated or else this luxury hotel was also part of the Bowman shop window.

In any case it had given Hannah a great deal of satisfaction. Exhausted as she had been last night from the long day's journey, she could still lift that elaborately coiffured head proudly and say, "This is how Ferdie and I did things, Emily. We neither wanted nor gave cut prices. I'm sorry, my dear, but you'll have to help me to bed."

"You miss Patterson," Emily said, easing the dress off the alarmingly thin old body.

"Miss her!" exclaimed Hannah. "On the contrary. This is the first time I seem to have escaped her for fifty years."

"Oh, surely, when you were with your husband—"

"Did she leave us then? I suppose she did. She always seems to have been around. Such devotion—or whatever it is." Hannah began her croaking chuckle. "She was furious when we left. Did you see her face? I believe she could have killed you for aiding and abetting that old fool Hannah Bowman in her craziness."

"I'm sure she could have." Emily laughed, but still felt traces of uneasiness.

It was not only Patterson who had disapproved of her going. Patterson had simply thought that such a journey would kill her mistress and that it had been Emily's duty

85

to flatly refuse to accompany her. That would have been the only way to dissuade her from her project. But Emily had none of Patterson's caution. If this was the way Hannah wanted to end her life, in the cut and thrust of her business and the high excitement of making new discoveries, then let her. She was no person for a long-drawn-out dull end. It would be very sad if she didn't get back to the *Casa de Flor*. Once, Dolly hadn't got back either, and that thought had been in both their minds on the long hot train journey yesterday. At least, Emily had been pretty sure it had been in Hannah's mind more than once. It certainly had been in her own.

It might have been in Patterson's, too. She had kept her worried fussing for Hannah, but for Emily she hadn't bothered to hide her hostility. It had been disconcerting, almost a little frightening, seeing that held-back anger in the round cosy face.

Patterson was not her friend, and never would be, for some reason.

Juana was a different matter.

She came bursting into Emily's room, crying, "Why are you taking Grandmama away?"

"I'm not taking her, honey, she's taking me."

"You are so taking her. Mummy said so. Won't you ever bring her back?"

Emily regarded the stormy little face with amusement and some tenderness. This undersized little creature viewed everything with the eyes of drama and usually of tragedy.

"Of course I'll bring her back."

Juana stared, fervently reading Emily's face.

"She won't be dead?"

"Good gracious, no!"

"Mummy said you'd kill her. I–I—"

"And you? What did you think?"

"I said you'd given me a handkerchief doll!" Juana burst out in an outraged attempt at fairness.

Emily held out her arms.

"Bless you, my pet!" The child, in her arms, had a bird's heart beating inside her frail chest. "Now listen. Will you practice that exercise I showed you while I'm away? Every day for half an hour. When I get back you can show me how well you can play it."

"Will you be back in time for my birthday?"

"I promise."

"That's on Saturday."

"We'll be back on Friday."

Juana withdrew with dignity.

"Then I'll go and tell Mummy to stop being so illogical."

"Juana, what an expression!"

"It's what Daddy said."

"Why did he say that?" Emily asked, hating herself.

"He said first you didn't want Emily, then you do, and Mummy said, what about you, and Daddy said, grow up, for God's sake, and kissed her to make her be quiet."

Already she's stealing my child. . . . Who was the neurotic, Juana or her mother?

There was also Fabrice to disapprove. It was quite clear he viewed the whole project with dismay. Apart from the danger to his mother's health he seemed to think she might do something exceedingly rash.

"Her judgment isn't what it was," he said, fixing his reproachful eyes on Emily. "If I can't persuade her against going, can't you? It really isn't wise, in her state of mind."

He seemed to be suggesting that Hannah was becoming senile. Emily was indignant.

"She's as sane as you or me."

Fabrice didn't remind her how short a time she had known Hannah. He was too courteous. He merely said, "You don't know all her characteristics. She's always had flashes of recklessness. My father curbed her, or her gambles came off. But will they now?"

"I'm the wrong person to ask. I have flashes of recklessness myself. I mean to defy the doctor and everyone else and give your mother this pleasure." Emily kissed Fabrice on his soft crumpled cheek. "Don't be such a worrier." His cheek was damp, a cool damp as if not from the heat, but some inner alarm, something not altogether to do with his mother's health.

Patrick said nothing. Or not to Emily. Perhaps because he never saw her alone. Lucie seemed to be always with him. And that was just as well. Emily tried to keep her eyes off him when he was in the room so that she wouldn't remember him too clearly when she was away. All the same, his face, or the echo of his voice, was in her mind too much. It was a good thing to escape from the *Casa de Flor* for a little while. These people had had a too violent impact on her. She must get them into perspective.

It was too early to ring for breakfast, and Hannah was

still asleep. Emily, to calm her excitement about the day ahead, and to try again to get things into perspective, sat down to write to her father.

There was so much to tell him.

"You can give up your cherished ideas that Hannah had anything to do with Dolly's death. She was too devoted to her, and still thinks of her constantly. Now I'm afraid she's transferring all that affection to me, and I'm not sure that this is a good thing although I also can't see how it can be a bad one. I think she's got some queer idea that I'm picking up life where poor Dolly left it off. But she's old and sick and all the family think she isn't quite in her right mind. That's why I still haven't talked a lot to her about Dolly's death. It distresses her too much, and Patterson, like a devoted old bulldog guarding her, won't allow that to happen.

"The family are all a bit suspicious of me for different reasons, especially now I've encouraged Hannah to have a final fling at Toledo today. The contents of an old Spanish palace are being sold and I can't tell you how excited I am to be there. Hannah, too. She has some deep dark plans. You won't like this, but I'm on Hannah's side already, she's a magnificent old woman. Really, Daddy, you'd admire her tremendously.

"For the rest, Fabrice is a darling, but rather an old fuddy-duddy. Patrick, Lucie's husband, is an artist, and sees nothing but his paintings, and his wife and child. Lucie is neurotic and has made Juana the same. I'm interfering madly, but can't help it. The infant is sweet when not in a tantrum.

"This is one thing Patrick and I agree on. Don't get the idea we disagree on others, he just has an absorbing talent, and wife, etc. etc. . . ."

And if she went on like this, her father would jump to the conclusion that she was in love with Patrick, and she would get a letter full of advice which she would have to tear up.

She thought of some more prosaic things with which to finish the letter, hastily sealed it and went downstairs to slip it in the postbox.

When she returned Hannah was awake and calling for her in a strangely feeble voice.

"Emily dear—most vexing—I'm afraid I feel quite unable to get up."

Emily bent over her in alarm.

"What is it? Shall I get a doctor?"

"No, no. It's only tiredness. The journey yesterday. I over-estimated my strength. I shall just have to rest. You'll have to go to Toledo without me."

"No, I'll stay with you."

"Bless you, dear, there's no need for that. I shall simply spend the day sleeping. I've ordered a car. The driver will take you. Now we've come this far, one of us must go. But how intolerably vexing. Are you familiar with the char-acteristics of a Rembrandt painting?"

"Only from the ones in the National Gallery."

"Do you think you could recognize one if you saw one? No, no, of course you couldn't be sure. Even an expert couldn't, without all those tests they do nowadays. Well, I don't suppose it is one. Anyway, this is my own fault, for wanting a last selfish triumph. I should have sent Patrick. Now it's too late. He'd never get here in time."

"Are you saying there might be a Rembrandt in the sale today?"

"Don Jaime told me long ago he had a painting that looked a little like one. I don't suppose for a moment it's true."

"But surely he'd have had it proved."

"Not this man. He just lived with the things that had always belonged to his family. Scarcely saw them, I imag-ine. He didn't need money. They said he'd become a re-ligious fanatic, as the Spaniards can."

"When did you meet him, Cousin Hannah?" Emily was asking.

Like an explosion in her brain the held-back picture came into focus.

Dolly on the railway station meeting that preposterous filthy train from Madrid. Dolly looking enchanting in a cream lace gown and an enormous lacy hat, and as miracu-lously cool as if no ray of that fiendish sun touched her, while Hannah, unsuitably dressed in her dark travelling clothes, achingly tired from having sat on wooden seats for hours, and suffering already from that too familiar form of travellers' torture, an upset stomach, could scarcely stand upright.

She blamed her migraine, her sick stomach, her aching bones, but the jealousy that swept over her as Dolly en-veloped her in a perfumed embrace and exclaimed in her delighted voice, "Hannah, have you come for my wedding?"

*had really begun in the first aware moment of her child-
hood. It merely culminated now, when she thought of that
horrible voluntary journey she had made to extricate Dolly
from her worst piece of foolishness, only to find the mad-
dening creature glowing with happiness. And lovely. Love-
lier than ever. . . .*

She hadn't realized how much she had hoped Dolly would
be in tears of distress and begging for help. Wouldn't any
other decent young woman be, after getting into the clutches
of a foreigner?

And such a foreigner. Hannah never believed Don Jaime
was real. Or real as he represented himself, an aristocrat who
lived in an ancient palace. She had none of Dolly's starry-
eyed trust in him.

"I met him in Seville," she told Hannah. "Some Spanish
friends of poor old Aunt Isabella's took me to a bullfight—"

"A bullfight!" Hannah exclaimed in horror.

"Oh, Hannah, that just shows how English you are. If you
live in Spain you have to go to bullfights."

"I have no intention of living in Spain," Hannah said tartly.
"Neither have you."

Dolly shot her a limpid glance.

"Well, anyway, I admit I was afraid I might faint, but I
didn't. It was all sort of poetically horrible. Jaime explained
about the poetry afterwards, and I did see what he meant.
He comes from Toledo. His family have a palace there, the
Palacio del Sol. We had dinner several times, with Aunt
Isabella's friends, of course, and once we went to a ball.
Then when I came back to Granada, Jaime followed me.
He said he loved me and wanted to marry me."

"His family, if they're that grand, would never let him."

Dolly gave her delighted laughter.

"Hannah, you haven't changed a bit, you're still wearing
your disapproving face. Relax now. You're in Spain. The
land of the pomegranates."

"You'd better come down to earth. I hope you haven't
been seeing this man unchaperoned."

"Of course I haven't. Patterson's been there, or the servants."

"You mean you've had him in your house!"

"My villa," said Dolly. "The Casa de Flor. Poor darling
Aunt Isabella saw how I loved it and that's why she left
it to me. I shall live here always."

"And what about the Palacio del Sol?" *Hannah asked ironically.*

"Oh, we shall go there for periods, of course. But this will be my favorite home."

Hannah didn't believe in the Palacio del Sol *any more than she did in Don Jaime. Perhaps he was a nobleman. He could just as easily have been a bullfighter. He had the dark intense eyes, the high-bridged nose and haughty expression of thousands of Spaniards who imagined themselves kings of the earth. He thought he could dominate everyone with his persuasive tongue and his charm. Silly susceptible Dolly might have been swept off her feet, but not Hannah.*

She decided at once to send the arrogant young man about his business. The Palacio del Sol, *indeed. If it existed. Wasn't it enough that Dolly had her small private fortune from that doting grandmother, and now the villa (and a most attractive one, Hannah grudgingly had to admit), from a doting aunt. Surely she didn't need a palace as well?*

The whole thing was utterly unsuitable, utterly unreliable. Don Jaime, the dashing Spaniard, had found a reckless English girl, not heavily chaperoned as were the women of his own country, and was amusing himself.

If he really meant to marry Dolly he would not have been so indiscreet. He knew of Dolly's fortune and intended to secure if for himself. So he made assignations in the Generalife Gardens at night, talking romantic nonsense about moonlight and nightingales.

What decent Spanish girl would have done such a thing? Hannah kept demanding of Dolly. Dolly smiled and said, "We must take you to the Palacio del Sol, *Hannah. I believe you think it's all made up."*

"I do," said Hannah curtly. For by that time she had found another reason to distrust Jaime.

If he had really meant to marry Dolly, if he really lived in a palace, it was all too utterly unfair for words, Dolly always getting riches of every kind handed to her.

And what was she, Hannah, to do, if this happened? Go back to England and find another governess's position? After finding how pleasant it was to have servants waiting on one.

And after meeting Ferdie. Ferdie had a tiny dark shop in the square. He sold a jumble of cheap rubbish, tourist things, dolls dressed as matadors or Flamenco dancers, castanets, gypsy costumes, and tambourines. Hannah had gone into the shop to buy picture postcards and had been impressed by Ferdie's earnest efforts to please. He would make a good businessman, she had thought. She had always known she would make a good business woman, given the opportunity.

Moreover, Ferdie seemed to look at her with admiration, and it couldn't have been because she looked like a rich foreigner. She may have looked foreign but certainly not rich. Ferdie had tried his halting English on her, and automatically she had corrected it. He had seized on this eagerly, explaining how anxious he was to learn. Perhaps she would have a cup of coffee with him and tell him some more.

This wasn't remotely like Dolly's indiscretion in going to dark gardens at night with a handsome braggadocio. It was merely sitting at a table in the square inhabited by a hundred other people in broad daylight, and speaking in slow painstaking English to an earnestly listening young man who wanted nothing but to improve himself.

This last emotion was one with which Hannah heartily sympathized. She had very little to do in Dolly's villa, so wasn't averse to the English lesson over coffee becoming a daily occurrence.

"I am visiting my rich cousin," she remembered saying, as Ferdie's understanding of her language improved.

Before very long Ferdie was regarding her as a friend, and then a close friend. Presently he delicately suggested in the Spanish that he was now teaching Hannah that he would like her to meet his family. And perhaps he could meet the rich cousin.

"I sell her something," he suggested merrily.

Hannah tactfully said that Dolly did most of her shopping in Madrid or Seville. And Ferdie, with that admirable ambition which Hannah admired so much, said why shouldn't there be a shop in Granada that people travelled from Seville and Madrid and even from other countries to visit.

Hannah said, "Yes, why not?" thoughtfully.

And the next day took Ferdie to the Casa de Flor to meet Dolly.

As it happened, he never did meet Don Jaime.

Later, when Dolly pointed out that Ferdie was low-class, and surely not the kind of person even Hannah would contemplate marrying, Hannah retorted that low-class or not, at least he was trustworthy. Not like Don Jaime. . . .

"When did you meet him, Cousin Hannah?" Emily asked

again. "Cousin Hannah! You're not listening."

The effort to come back to the present was growing more and more difficult.

"When? Oh, years ago. Ferdie and I used to go to some affairs in Madrid. We met clients that way. I tried to interest Don Jaime in a religious carving. A Gil de Siloe, I believed, though we couldn't prove it. You'll see his work in some of the old cathedrals in Spain. But Don Jaime wasn't interested in acquiring anything. Nor in selling. A pity. And now," Hannah moved fretfully on the pillows, "when my opportunity comes I can't take it. You'll have to be my eyes. Come back and tell me everything—everything."

Emily began to wonder if once Hannah had been in love with the mysterious austere Don Jaime. The discovery of a Rembrandt would be terrific, and solve all Hannah's financial worries. But Emily didn't think she had any real belief in the picture in question being such an exciting thing. Her desire to wander through that old palace seemed more personal, as if she had long been denied the opportunity.

She was staring thoughtfully at the dark painting when Patrick's voice behind her said, "It isn't, you know."

Emily spun round, her breath held.

"It isn't a Rembrandt, as Hannah hoped it might be."

"How did you know? What are you doing here?"

"About the Rembrandt?" said Patrick. "Patterson, the keeper of the mistress's secrets, Hannah's conscience, you might almost say, told me. And what am I doing here? Do you think I'd let Hannah go off the way she is, without keeping an eye on her? It was no use coming with you. She wouldn't have allowed that."

Nor Lucie, Emily thought. Lucie certainly wouldn't have allowed it if she had been permitted to speak. Perhaps this time she had been kept silent. Patrick had simply said he was coming, and here he was, sunburnt, a little tired about the eyes, serious, concerned. But here, within touching distance.

"So I followed by car," he said. "I drove all night. Nice old castle this, isn't it? Partly Moorish, did you notice? Where is Hannah? Sitting down somewhere?"

"No, that's just it. She was feeling too tired to come. I left her in bed at the hotel. I can hear Patterson saying, 'Didn't I tell you!' But Hannah insisted on my coming here today. It was going to upset her more if I stayed with her than if I left her. She said I had to be her eyes."

"Then you'd better let me show you what's worth seeing. On the whole I find the stuff extraordinarily dull. Hannah's saved herself a wasted journey."

"What about that?" asked Emily, pointing to a portrait. "It looks like a Goya."

"Same fashion. Goya had his copyists just as Rembrandt had. I should imagine the gentlemen in that portrait is one of Don Jaime's ancestors."

"He looks vaguely familiar," said Emily. "I feel as if I've met him somewhere."

"You can't have. He's probably been dead a hundred years."

Emily caught Patrick's arm, delaying him as he was moving on.

"He's like Fabrice!" She was triumphant at identifying the resemblance. "Those dark melancholy eyes and the heavy jowls. Isn't he?"

"Impossible!" Patrick narrowed his eyes, looking at the portrait. It was a little while before he said, "A lot of Spaniards look alike. Black eyes, olive complexion."

"Then Fabrice must take after his father. He's not a bit like Hannah. Did you know Ferdie?"

"No, he'd died before I met the family. But Hannah always said the Spanish side had come out in her children."

"They're not alike—Fabrice and Lucie."

"Not in temperament, no." Patrick didn't enlarge on that. His eyes had darkened. He was thinking of Lucie and her inexplicable moods. Though were they inexplicable to him? He walked away from the portrait that really did have an odd haunting resemblance to Fabrice, and Emily overcame the temptation to ask him how it was Lucie had allowed him to come to Toledo today. She wanted to live utterly in this happiness that had begun, exploding inside her like a light the moment she had heard Patrick's voice. She had said calm and sedate things to him. It had been as if someone else were talking while all the time she, the real Emily, was cherishing her feeling of transfiguration.

Oh, lord, she must concentrate on practical things, the portrait that looked like Fabrice, the amazing symmetry of the mosaic flooring they were walking on, the tapestried walls, the sun striking golden across an open doorway, the heavy Spanish furniture marked with lot numbers, the chauffeur waiting for her in the shade of the courtyard, Hannah's disappointment when she was told the picture was not a Rembrandt (though had she really expected it to be one—or had that been a colorful device to cover another reason for making this reckless journey?).

"Do you think Don Jaime was an old lover of Hannah's?" Emily asked. "And that this was merely a sentimental journey?"

"Before Ferdie?" Patrick was interested.

"Perhaps. But I don't see her. Hannah was heavily disguised as a governess then. I think it would have to have been after Ferdie. She says how he developed her looks and her personality. But falling in love with someone else hardly fits in with her devotion to Ferdie, does it?"

"That could be caused by guilt."

"You say that as if you know too much about guilt," Emily said, and had a sudden wincing vision of him taking flowers to Lucie's grave every week faithfully for the rest of his life. The chill little picture seemed to go with the mood of this ancient castle and its feeling of past dramas.

"I don't know about Hannah's guilt. She has plenty, I should think, one way and another, the old devil."

Patrick was laughing, but just for a moment he had looked as if he carried an intolerable burden, something that made him sympathise with Hannah's possible transgressions.

Spontaneously Emily took his hand.

"Let's go out in the sun."

"Your hand's cold!"

"I always shiver in castles."

"Have you seen Toledo?"

"Only in the distance this morning."

"Then let's go there for lunch and I'll show it to you."

"But I ought to get back to Hannah. I've got a car waiting, too."

"We'll send the car back. We'll telephone Hannah from Toledo to make sure she's all right. Now you've made the required protests. So come along and share my guilt."

"Then you do have it!"

"I ought to be at home working."

"Oh, that! Then let's go," Emily cried.

It was impossible to remain out in the noon sun. They lunched at a white-clothed table in a courtyard heavily shaded by a grape-vine trellis. Emily sipped the cool white wine, and looked at Patrick and felt the happiness wash over her. Tomorrow her caution, if she had any left, would return.

"What guilt?" she said. "Not just because of a day off work. Not just being with me?"

"I was joking." He looked happier now, the shadow gone from his eyes. "I feel nothing, at this minute, but contentment."

"Oh, I feel more than that," said Emily, hugging her arms ecstatically round herself.

"What do you feel?" His voice was lazy.

"I don't know—as if I'm bursting with joy. It's what music does to me. It's utter bliss to find something else can do it, too. I feel whole again. Do you understand?"

"And what is making you whole now, Emily? Just Toledo, an ancient pile of stones?"

"No, it's everything, the sun on my arm here, the way the shadows are so black on the white stone, the taste of the food, you, I suppose—"

"You have the enthusiasms of a little girl."

"Oh, I know. I get carried away. They say I'm like my Aunt Dolly. They say she fell in love with everything in Spain, even the wrong man—"

Automatically their eyes met.

"You mustn't do that, Emily."

"No, no, it would be crazy."

"Quite crazy."

"You hated me when I arrived." She couldn't help it. This ground was dangerous, but she had to tread on it. "I could see it in your face. You'd have liked to send me right back to England. You were so angry."

"That," said Patrick frowning, "is the way I am quite a lot of the time. No, I didn't hate you. Far from it. I only saw at once that you would be another complication."

"As far as Juana was concerned?"

"Not only Juana."

She persisted crazily, "Who else?"

"Come off it, Emily. You're too intelligent to need to ask that question. You look in a mirror occasionally, I take it."

She was ashamed of herself. "I'm sorry. I understand. You mean Lucie's jealous."

"Lucie is always jealous. It's her Spanish temperament, I suppose."

"You should be pleased that she loves you so much."

"Love? Is that love? I try to believe it is, but I can think of other names for it. Fear, repression, loneliness."

"She couldn't be lonely with you!" Emily burst out.

He gave a half smile.

"Speak for yourself, Emily. Are you speaking for yourself?"

Her nod was the merest inclination of her head, but suddenly he looked pleased and didn't try to hide his pleasure.

"Well, that doesn't mean Lucie feels the same way, and we have to think of her."

We. The word joined them together. Emily nodded earnestly, knowing her unhappiness later would still make this conversation worth while.

"But don't let's waste this day on my problems," Patrick said. "It's bad luck for Lucie, being the way she is, that you're so pretty. But pleasant for me. I like to look at you. One day I'll paint you. And I think you're giving Juana a necessary balance between a neurotic mother and an angry father. Now let's have some more wine. Then we'll go and see the famous El Greco in the Church of Sante Tome. And you might like to buy a Toledo sword. Useful for possible murders."

Emily was grateful to him for skirting the dangerous emotional mood she had evoked. This was how it was to be, indeed the only way it could be. But she could still keep the lovely golden day.

"What did Hannah say when you talked to her on the telephone just now?"

"I told you. She said, 'Take care of Emily.' "

"Oh, bless her. She's so kind to me. But half the time she's mixed up and thinks I'm Dolly. She must have loved Dolly. My father was quite wrong about all that."

"Oh?" Patrick was interested. "Why?"

"He always blamed Hannah for letting Dolly die. Seemed to think it was carelessness, or worse. Daddy's got what one might call a Gothic imagination. Oh, I know! While I'm in Madrid I must go and see Dolly's grave."

"Isn't that morbid?"

"No one has ever bothered," Emily said heatedly. "Her parents were those sort of Victorian people who were scared to travel to foreign countries. They thought they'd die of some bug. So poor Dolly has always been neglected. Except for Hannah, of course. I must do that. I must ask Hannah where it is."

The drive back to Madrid was the last enchantment. The low hills rose in dusky curves against the sunset sky, the strings of laden donkeys were plodding home behind their barefooted owners, the women were coming from the fields, the white handkerchiefs, shields against the fierce sun, still tied round their heads. The sky faded from yellow to apple green. The ghost grey eucalyptus and olive trees merged into the landscape. The heat still lingered.

Hannah was up and sitting in a chair at the window when they came into her room.

"Well?" she said. Her topaz eyes, heavy-lidded, went over them. Her face didn't change, but Emily suddenly had the guilty feeling that they had come in hand in hand. It was how she had wanted to come in and she supposed it was written in her face. "So it wasn't a Rembrandt?"

"No, Mamita love, and you didn't expect it to be."

"One hardly expects that kind of luck, I admit. What did you think of it all, Emily?" Her keen gaze concentrated on Emily alone.

"I thought Toledo was fabulous."

"No, no, no, not Toledo, the *Palacio del Sol.*"

"It was interesting, but somehow"—She didn't know why she suddenly shivered—"I can't imagine anyone who wasn't born to it wanting to live in a place like that."

Hannah settled back in her chair.

"No. One would have to be born to it. That's what I always said."

"Why, Cousin Hannah? Did *you* contemplate living there?"

"*I!* What an extraordinary suggestion."

"There was a portrait there that I thought looked like Fabrice."

For a moment she was afraid her impulsive tongue had made a bad blunder. A swift look of cold hauteur had passed over Hannah's face. But it was gone immediately, and Hannah began to laugh loudly and enjoyably.

"Fabrice an aristocrat! Now that we mustn't dare to tell him, otherwise he'll never sell another thing. Did you think this, Patrick? Or was it just Emily's wild imagination?"

"It was a typical Spanish face," said Patrick. "I suppose it might have looked like Fabrice the way Emily might look like the young Lady Hamilton."

"Exactly," said Hannah. "Sit down, children. Well, Patrick, you naughty boy, so you won't trust me out of your sight. What did Lucie have to say to this?"

"Lucie said if you wanted to kill yourself, who was I to stop you? But I will stop you, if it's humanly possible."

"And take Emily sight-seeing in the process?"

"Is there any law against that?" Patrick's eyes glinted.

"One or two I can think of. Well, never mind now. Emily looks as if the sun has caught her, and she could do with some rest. We'll leave for home tomorrow."

"We'll go by car," said Patrick. "We'll stop overnight at Cordoba and Emily can see the mosque."

"This was a business trip," Hannah said crossly. "You're turning it into a junket."

"You wanted Emily to see something of Spain. What better opportunity? Oh, and by the way, Emily would like to visit Dolly's grave while she's in Madrid. Where is it, Mamita? I can take her there in the morning."

Dolly's grave. . . .

The sound of the train clattering on its infinitely tedious journey towards Madrid, night falling and rain misting on the dirty windows. . . . It never rained, it was never cold in Castille, yet here she was shivering violently as the smoky air stirred in cold draughts, freezing her neck and giving her a sharp ache in one shoulder.

The train was already two hours late. Hannah was so tired that Dolly's face was hazy. Dolly's voice wasn't very clear either, or perhaps that was because she didn't want to hear it.

"Hannah! Hannah, how far are we from Toledo now?"

She had to rouse because Dolly was nudging her awake, and the tormented little face was looking up into hers.

"I've told you a thousand times, we aren't going to Toledo."

"Oh!" The flat disappointment in Dolly's voice made fierce anger surge through Hannah, turning her chilliness to a sweating heat.

"Dolly, for goodness' sake, where is your pride? I can only make allowances because you are ill. Never mind, dear." She softened her voice anxiously. "We'll soon be there now. Try to rest."

Dolly sighed deeply and appeared to settle to doze, her head slipping on to Hannah's shoulder. Hannah couldn't move now, and the pain in her shoulder became agonizing. She gave an unguarded moan and Dolly struggled up.

"Hannah, what's the matter? You look ill."

"I have a little chill. It's nothing."

"Are you sure?" Involuntarily Dolly moaned herself. *"W*
can't have your baby born on a train. What a furore!" She
chuckled faintly in a way that sounded slightly delirious, and
Hannah roused herself to stroke the girl's sweat-dampened
forehead. Dolly was right. It would be dreadful to have the
baby born on the train. She calmly assured Dolly that no
such thing would happen, but Dolly seemed to be beyond
hearing. She lay back, her blue eyes glazed, the high color
burning in her cheeks.

Much later she said clearly, *"I'll have my revenge one
day."*

They were the last coherent words she said before the
tardy lights of Madrid came into sight. . . .

"Cousin Hannah! You have that queer look again. Are
you feeling worse?" That was Emily's anxious voice. Emily's
healthy face above her clarified and was infinitely welcome
and reassuring. Dear Emily! No such nightmare train jour-
neys for her.

"Emily only wanted to know where Dolly's grave is, Mamita."

"Yes, and she made me remember. Everything about coming here has made me remember." Hannah turned her head
restlessly on the pillow. "No, Emily dear, you mustn't go
near it. The English don't understand Spanish cemeteries.
This one is like a sort of awful filing cabinet, the dead
tucked away in layers. No, it's too painful, Emily. I beg
you not to go. I went only once. It's why I insisted on
Ferdie having a plot of his own and a proper headstone.
But Dolly was—put away—while I was still so ill myself.
I had no voice in the matter. Leave it, Emily. It will only
distress me. Besides, if we're to reach Cordoba tomorrow we
must make an early start."

"Of course, Cousin Hannah, if you'd hate it," Emily said.

"I would hate it, and so would you. Say no more about
it. Dolly will understand."

On the verge of sleep, Emily was aware of Hannah, a
gaunt figure leaning on her stick, at her bedside.

"Emily, it won't do, you know."

Emily thought the old lady was wandering, talking in her
sleep.

"What won't do?"

"You can't fall in love with Patrick. You'll only be terribly
unhappy."

"But I haven't, Cousin Hannah."

"I'm glad to hear it."

"All the same, this was the loveliest day I ever had. Thanks to you, Cousin Hannah."

"Ha! But this wasn't the way I meant it to go. I want you to be happy."

Emily thought of the day ahead, the road winding through the red hills to Cordoba, and said that she was blissfully happy.

"I don't know why you're so kind to me. I don't know why you should mind so much whether I'm happy or not."

"Let's put it down to an old woman's whim. No, it's more than that. It goes back to Dolly, as you must know. I saved her from one unhappy love affair, but I didn't know she would die before she could have another. If I'd known she was going to die"—Hannah's face was gaunt and very old—"then I'd not have interfered. I'd have let her live while she could."

"So I'm your Dolly," Emily said gently.

Hannah nodded, not denying this impractical and ever so slightly morbid fact.

"That's why I don't want you to get hurt. I saw the way you looked at Patrick tonight."

"He loves Lucie," Emily said.

"Lucie loves him." It seemed as if Hannah were correcting her. "What's more, Lucie was brought up as a Catholic. She'd never divorce him. And there's Juana."

"Cousin Hannah, you don't need to give me a lecture. Patrick came today because he was worried about you, not me. And you ought to be in bed, not standing there. Anyway," she was contradicting herself now, "did you never do anything reckless, a thing that swept you away and you knew there could never possibly be anything more important at that time—even if you paid afterwards?"

"Now you're talking like Dolly," Hannah said harshly. "It won't do, Emily. If you're going to be foolish I'll have to send you back to London."

"I won't be foolish, Cousin Hannah. I think Patrick's terribly attractive, but every time I look at him I see Lucie at his shoulder. You don't need to worry. All the same," she finished bitterly, "why doesn't Lucie trouble to make him happier if she loves him so much?"

"That's not your business, Emily. Don't try to make it so. Otherwise there'll be more trouble in that house, and there's been enough already. More than enough," Hannah added under her breath. "Though I suppose I should have known —resurrecting Dolly—Patterson warned me—"

Emily sat up, a little alarmed at Hannah's slurring voice. She was speaking as if against her will, as if some old grievance were driving her.

"What are you saying, Cousin Hannah? I don't understand any of this. I think you're too obsessed with Dolly. She seems more alive to you than if she were really here. I might look like her, but I'm not going to wear her shoes. The mistakes I make will be my own, and if I fall in love it will be me, *me,* falling in love, not Dolly."

"Oh, my lamb, don't be foolish. You make me afraid!"

"What of? What of?"

But Hannah had shuffled slowly away, as if exhausted. Or as if she couldn't trust herself to say anything more.

Emily knew better than to call her back. One day all these half-told things would fit together. Now Emily was certain that Dolly and Hannah had had a dreadful quarrel, and Hannah had been living with her remorse ever since. The visit to the *Palacio del Sol* today and the mysterious Don Jaime had something to do with it. And Hannah's reluctance for Emily to visit Dolly's grave. And her great desire for Emily's happiness which would somehow wipe out the memory of the tears poor Dolly had shed.

She was certain Hannah would tell her the whole story one day.

In the meantime, there was tomorrow, tomorrow, tomorrow. . . . Who ever could expect her to be cautious!

CHAPTER TEN

THE telephone buzzed beside Emily's bed before she was awake. She started up, looking at her watch. It was just seven o'clock. A vague feeling of alarm stirred in her as she picked up the receiver.

"A call from Granada for you, senorita," said the operator, and immediately following came Lucie's voice, high-pitched and urgent.

"Is that you, Emily? Will you tell my husband he's got to come home immediately? Juana's ill."

"Oh, I'm sorry. Very ill?"

"Of course she's very ill or I wouldn't be ringing. The doctor was here twice yesterday and he's coming again this morning. She's had one of her worst attacks, and it's only because her father's disappeared, and her grandmother. She doesn't understand it."

Oh, come off it, Lucie, the child's eight years old. You mean you haven't explained it to her. Or you've deliberately confused her and upset her.

"Emily! Did you hear what I said?"

"Yes, I did. And we're setting out for home today. But we planned to stay the night in Cordoba. I don't think your mother could travel all the way without a rest."

"Then she had no business to go on this crazy trip," Lucie cried. "You should never have encouraged her. You and Patrick."

"Certainly I encouraged her," Emily said. "When you're getting near the end of your life wouldn't you like to be allowed to do the things that matter to you? We can't argue about this on the telephone, Lucie, but it isn't fair to say Patrick encouraged her, too. He merely came to keep an eye on her."

"Oh, is that what he's doing?" Lucie said in her distraught voice. "Are you sure? Don't tell me he hasn't taken you to see the sights in Toledo. I can just see Mama climbing about those cobbled streets."

"Hadn't you better speak to your husband yourself?" Emily said stiffly.

"No, no, I'll only be told I fuss unnecessarily about Juana, even though the doctor warns me that another attack today would be dangerous. Can I tell Juana you're on your way?"

"Yes."

"How is Mama?" Lucie asked belatedly.

"Tired, but well."

"I can rely on you, Emily?"

What is it you mean, you witch? Can you rely on me not to let Patrick enjoy himself, not to let the strain ease out of his face, not to let him forget that he ought to feel guilty all the time?

"You can rely on me," she said drily.

"Emily, who are you talking to?" came Hannah's voice from the next room.

Emily got out of bed and went in to see Hannah.

"Lucie. She says Juana's ill."

Hannah's eyes narrowed. "She wants Patrick back."

"Yes. She says Juana's fretting."

"We can make a guess who's fretting."

"Then you don't think Juana's illness is serious?"

"Would she have told you instead of Patrick?" Hannah's voice was sardonic. "No, it won't be any more serious than usual. But that's bad enough. I suppose everyone at some time has the temptation to wield power over another person, but to do it over a child! It worries me, Emily. That child has to be saved from being destroyed by her parents."

"Both of them?" Emily said involuntarily.

"Both of them. Quarrels, dramas, both of them with inflammable tempers. Well, you'd better let Patrick know we're to make an early start."

But Patrick, even at that early hour, could not be found. He was not in his room, nor apparently in the hotel. At the hour they had arranged to leave, nine o'clock, he appeared, and although he hadn't been told of Lucie's call he already looked *distrait*. He said he had been getting the car attended to and had breakfasted at a café. It was a lovely morning, but promised to be very hot later. They had better get as far on their way as possible before the real heat began.

"And before Lucie tweaks your tail again," said Hannah drily.

"Lucie!"

"She rang me up," Emily said reluctantly. "Juana's been ill. She wants you home."

Patrick stared a moment, his eyes hardening.

"And she couldn't tell me this herself?"

That was something Emily could spare him.

"How could she, when you were out?"

"The women in this family aren't always predictable. Are they, Mamita darling? Enigmas, all of you."

"All of us, Patrick? How many do you count? Lucie, me. Emily, too?" There was the briefest flicker of something in her eyes as she looked at Patrick and he made no answer. She went on in her dry voice, "I am quite happy to be an enigma. But I would have thought Lucie all too obvious. And Emily, bless her, couldn't deceive a child." She moved impatiently. "Well—why are we standing here? With the sun promising to scorch us off the road, with that child obediently breaking her heart for her father, have we time to waste?"

Patrick opened the door of the car, and helped Hannah in. Emily followed. She knew already that there was going to be no charm in this day.

"But aren't you worried about Juana?" she had to ask.

"No more than usual. Am I right, Mamita?"

"You're right to be worried." Hannah's voice was harsh. "Let's get home. This trip was a mistake, after all. We should have listened to the others, Emily. Fabrice will say there was no business done, Patterson will say I look at death's door, and Lucie—we know what Lucie's saying. You and Patrick—but Patrick wasn't part of my plan."

"What was your plan, Mamita?" Patrick's voice wasn't off-hand enough to disguise deep interest. "It wasn't the supposed Rembrandt. If you had thought there was any chance of that being genuine you'd have asked me to go and look at it."

"I wanted to make the discovery myself," Hannah said sulkily. "A last fling, if you like."

"Sounds nice, but I don't believe you."

Hannah's face had its basilisk expression. "It's the truth. But you must make allowances for my senility."

"Senile! You!" Emily cried.

"Ask Patterson," said Hannah. "That old devil allows me no illusions."

"Then it must have been sentimentality," Patrick said, and again something flickered in Hannah's eyes. Was it fear? Suddenly Emily was remembering the portrait that had looked like Fabrice.

"Anyway, it was a mistake," said Hannah, after a long time. Then she fell silent. So did Patrick.

The heat mounted as the road wound ahead of them through the dry red hills. After an hour or so of seeming to doze Hannah opened her eyes, but seemed alarmingly tired. When Emily asked if she felt able to continue the journey she shrugged, saying, "If it kills me, I suppose it will be what I deserve. After all, I killed Dolly doing just this."

"You didn't, Cousin Hannah!"

The old head nodded tiredly. "Your father wasn't so far wrong, after all. It's haunted me enough all these years. If I hadn't insisted on trying to get her to the hospital in

Madrid she might not have died. I truly thought it was the wisest thing to do—but how can one know?"

"If you're going to sin," said Patrick over his shoulder, "do it with panache. Your own words, Mamita. Don't start spoiling them with remorse."

Abruptly Hannah gave her appreciative croak of amusement. "You should have been my son, Patrick. You understand me."

"I am your son, Mamita. And much good it does us all."

By lunchtime they found a hotel where Hannah could rest, lying down in a darkened room, while Emily and Patrick had some food, stringy cold chicken and salad, and coffee, at a table under a dusty acacia tree outside.

The little square was full of the usual loungers, old men sitting in the shade, young men leaning against walls and staring. Their liquid dark eyes never moved from Emily.

"Does it upset you?" Patrick asked. "You should be flattered."

But to Emily, suddenly, all the dark staring eyes were Lucie's eyes. There you sit falling in love with my husband, they said. It's no use. He's mine. Juana binds us.

"Do you think Hannah will be all right?" she asked, determining to be impersonal.

"I hope so. It's going to be hot this afternoon. They say Cordoba is the frying pan of Spain. But Hannah's used to the heat. What about you? You're not used to it."

"Oh, don't worry about me. I'm tough."

"Are you, Emily?"

"Yes," she said, meeting his probing gaze.

"Then why did you let Lucie's call upset you? If you're tough you wouldn't let other people's unhappiness rub off on you."

"I'm upset about Juana," Emily said defensively.

"Naturally. You think we're tearing her to bits."

"Why does Lucie *do* this?"

Patrick stirred his coffee. His head was bent. His cheekbones beneath the sun-browned skin looked too prominent.

"Lucie's methods get monotonous. You must have noticed that by now."

"You said unhappiness a little while ago."

"That's the word. Don't ask me why. I suppose it's my fault. God knows, I've tried. Well—the old Spanish proverb has it—'Love doth pain sometimes but it never slayeth.' We're still alive. If I have a successful exhibition I'll take

Lucie to Paris. She can have a shopping spree."

"Will that cure anything?"

"Of course it won't. But it will get us through another few weeks of our life. Now don't say life isn't meant to be just got through. And don't look at me like that."

Emily's nerves were as raw as his. "I'm not looking at you with pity. You, a grown man, you should be able to manage your life better!"

Quickly she added, "No, I didn't mean that. Forgive me," but he, looking at her as persistently and unashamedly as the inquisitive Spaniards, was saying softly:

"Maybe I will, Emily. Maybe I will."

Then he sprang up. "Come along, we'd better see how Hannah is, and get on our way. What's the matter, are you sad to leave your admirers?"

Emily tried to laugh. She was far from sorry to leave the interested audience lounging about the square. But Patrick was too observant. She would have to be more careful. The shaft of pain at the thought of he and Lucie having a reconciliation in Paris had caught her too sharply to hide it. Her emotions were getting too dangerous.

At Cordoba, Hannah made her go and see the mosque. It was fantastic and beautiful, but its shadowy distances seemed vaguely sinister. She was imagining tragedies much older than lovely Dolly's death on the way to Madrid. She felt lost and lonely, and knew that Patrick hadn't come with her because his emotions were getting out of hand, too. He would be making himself think of the reconciliation he and Lucie were going to have in Paris, presumably while Emily kept Juana happy.

As she came out of the dusky haunted avenues of the mosque into the blazing yellow light of late afternoon, a small boy gave her a red rose. He grinned widely, hoping for a peseta. The pretty, if mercenary, act cheered her. She tucked the rose into her dress and went back to the hotel where she found Patrick perched on a stool at the bar, drinking vermouth and soda, and sketching the barman on the back of the wine list.

"So you're surrendering to the charm of the Spanish, I see," he said, looking at the rose in her bosom.

"I'm hot and thirsty. You were quite right that I shouldn't miss the mosque. It's fabulous but it seemed full of the ghosts of old crimes."

"Yes, the Moors were clever with scimitars. You should have bought that sword in Toledo."

"Why?"

There had been an undercurrent in his voice that she didn't understand.

"To be forearmed—"

"You mean, to be forewarned."

"So I do. Have a drink. A long, cool drink."

"What are you warning me about?"

"What am I warning you about? Making mistakes. Getting too involved with us. Hannah's dangerous senility."

"You don't believe that!"

"No." He twirled his glass, chinking the ice against the sides. "If she's senile, she has been for a very long time. Fifty years, perhaps."

Emily took his arm impatiently.

"*What* are you telling me?"

His eyes were as inscrutable as Hannah's.

"Only that she's a devious old woman. I'm not sure what's going to happen. But something is going to happen. And the thing is, I don't know whether she means it to, or not."

"You found out something in Madrid!" Emily exclaimed. When he didn't answer she went on, "Or in Toledo."

"Yes, I did. In Toledo I found that you were too beautiful for any man's peace of mind, and in Madrid I made the same discovery all over again."

"You're prevaricating!"

"What a word to use on a hot day. My dear little old-fashioned Emily."

"Be serious! You are underneath, I know. Tell me what you're warning me about."

"Everything. But everything. Hannah, Lucie, Fabrice, me." He beat his breast. "Me, me, me!"

"Patrick! You've had a drink too many."

"And you one too few. Sorry, Emily." He lifted haggard eyes. "I wanted to show you the mosque, but I came here and telephoned my wife instead."

"And—it's all right?"

"It will be better when we arrive home." He said something in Spanish to the barman, which seemed to mean that the man was to hurry with Emily's drink. "And we convince her that we're not lovers," he added.

Emily stared at him, her eyes widened.

"Well, are we?" he asked.

She took the ice-cold glass the barman put in front of her gratefully. She had a long swallow of the refreshing drink before she said, "I hope this isn't the sort of conversation you had with Lucie."

"I suppose I said the same thing in different words. Juana's still ill. Or so she says."

"Do you think she is?"

"No. But I can't be sure."

"Patrick, you're frowning." It wasn't what she had meant to say at all. But the deep line scored between his eyes hurt her physically. He must stop doing that.

The barman had gone out through a door at the back of the bar. Patrick leaned forward and kissed Emily, first on her brow, where perhaps she was frowning herself, then on her lips. His touch was soft, almost passionless. She noticed his hands were clenched.

He said lightly, "That's because of your yellow hair." He took her hand and kissed each finger separately. "And not to be remembered," he said, sliding off his stool and going with his quick stride towards the door.

She had to finish her drink alone. She did that quickly, before she began to cry into it, and the barman thought her drunk.

They reached home in the late afternoon the following day. Juana came running out to meet them.

She flung herself into Patrick's arms, then kissed her grandmother dutifully. She hung back from Emily, saying, in a rush, "I couldn't practice on the piano. Truly I couldn't. Mummy wouldn't let me because I was sick."

"Were you sick?" Patrick demanded.

"Yes, I was, but not very. Mummy said I must stay in bed so I'd be well for my birthday."

"Juana! Come out of the sun!" That was Lucie's voice, and the next moment Lucie appeared, slim and elegant in an immaculate white dress, but with just the faintest look of dishevelment about her, her hair slightly disordered, her lipstick carelessly put on.

"So you're home," she said, making no move to come forward and welcome them. Her arms went round Juana protectively. "She's better today, so now I suppose you won't believe how ill she was yesterday."

"Hello, Lucie," said Patrick, kissing her on the cheek.

Lucie's face contracted. Her enormous liquid eyes had a shine that looked like tears.

"Well, aren't you going to say you're glad to see me back alive?" said Hannah drily. "After all those dire forebodings of yours and Patterson's."

"It was Patrick who had the forebodings. Or so he said." Lucie's eyes flicked over Emily. "I don't think he had much faith in your commonsense, Emily. I hope he was wrong."

"Actually he was right," Emily said coolly. "I have no commonsense at all."

There, she had told Lucie what she wanted to know. She had fallen in love with Patrick, it was no use denying it any longer. But Patrick—a glance at his face showed the now familiar tension and exasperation. Lucie, be careful, she wanted to say. If you really love your husband, don't taunt him too far. Can't you feel the violence he's been damming down for so long?

"I don't know what you're all talking about," Hannah said irritably. "I've found Emily to be perfectly sensible and reliable. She has looked after me splendidly. If you could look after your child as well, Lucie, things would be much better. Now I must go in and sit down. Patterson—where's Patterson?"

"Oh, Patterson—I should warn you, Mama. She's got a visitor. He arrived yesterday."

"He! Who?" Hannah's face was stone.

"Her nephew. The wonderful Raymond. Fabrice and I had to entertain him to dinner last night. I must say it's a bit off. One doesn't expect it of old Patterson."

Hannah, tapping her stick noisily on the mosaic paving, made her way to the house. Some emotion, it looked very like fury, had made her forget her exhaustion. It seemed as if the discreet Patterson had overstepped the mark at last.

Hannah could scarcely wait to get to her room. There she rang her bell noisily, not stopping until Patterson appeared, out of breath.

"There, madam! I knew how it would be. You arriving home exhausted and in a tantrum."

"A tantrum is scarcely the word, Patterson. How dare you invite your nephew into my house! That's the height of insolence. I won't stand it."

"But, madam!" Patterson's expression was full of surprise. "I told you he was planning a visit to Granada this summer.

I suddenly thought, Why wait until the worst of the heat? and sent off a telegram suggesting he come now. Mind you, I didn't think he would arrive quite so soon. But that shows how keen he is, doesn't it?"

Hannah controlled her anger sufficiently to ask, "Keen on what?"

"Why, everything, madam. The architecture, the food, a bit of love, too, I wouldn't be surprised." Patterson chuckled comfortably. "He's young and we all know what Spain can do to the young, don't we?"

Color suffused Hannah's face. She struggled for coherence.

"So the moment my back was turned you deliberately brought your nephew here, installing him in my house, having him at my table! Oh, no, Patterson, you've gone too far this time. You'll get that unprincipled youth out of here immediately, and you'll go with him."

Patterson was a statue, her stone grey eyes unflickering.

"Did I hear right, madam? Are you dismissing me?"

"Yes, I am. I should have done it years ago. How I've endured your tyranny for so long I'll never know."

"But you find my tyranny indispensable, madam," Patterson said softly.

Hannah clenched her hands.

"Don't use words you've learned from me. You're a servant. Talk like a servant."

Patterson ignored that as a piece of irrelevance.

"Who would help you to dress, madam? And get you in and out of your bath?" (See your skinny unlovely body, your hair straggling, your face sagging, were her unspoken words.) "Your kind niece who thinks you're so wonderful when you're all dolled up in your Chanel dresses? It's not a job for her, madam. Finding out all your nasty secrets, eh?" Her unblinking eyes stared at Hannah. "No, this is my job. We've grown old together. Me leave you! Excuse me, madam, but you're talking nonsense!"

Hannah had to sit down because she could not stand any longer. She looked at the stout figure in front of her. It was quite immovable. Like a mountain. A volcanic mountain, sometimes spitting burning lava. Dangerous. . . .

"Get rid of the boy!" she whispered. "That's too much. Even from—such an old servant." Her voice was exhausted. She knew that this was her worst defeat. She had to whip herself into a semblance of her old biting sarcasm. "How did you find your loving nephew after all these years? A spotty gauche youth full of inflated opinions, I've no doubt."

"He knows what he wants," Patterson said with infuriating smugness. "I think you'll be quite impressed by him, madam."

"Oh, I expect he knows how to flatter. I'm not taken in by flattery—like most old women." She let that barb sink in, then asked, "How long is he planning to stay?"

"I'm not sure, madam. As long as he finds Granada interesting, I should think. But I've already told him he can't expect to live on your hospitality. So don't fret yourself. You get into a state over nothing. Raymond will find himself a room somewhere. After all, he's only a student and students don't expect to live in luxury."

"Don't they?" Hannah commented with all the irony she could muster.

"Of course not, madam. Raymond is very sensible. And very grateful to be able to stay here a night or two while he finds his way about." Patterson stood over her, ready, now she had won the major battle, to make concessions. "I suppose you think I took a liberty, madam, asking Raymond to come like this. It was seeing you with Miss Emily that did it. I'm flesh and blood, too. I suddenly wanted to see someone of my own family. It's been a long time since I did. Not since we were in London when Raymond was only a little lad. Now he's a grown man. And so clever, you couldn't believe it."

"Oh, I'd believe it."

"Yes, he's already taught me a thing or two."

"Then let him confine himself to your education, Patterson. I don't think Emily will be particularly interested in lectures on architecture—or anything else. If that's the little scheme you had in mind."

"If you don't mind my saying so, madam, it would be better for Miss Emily to listen to my nephew than what she's been doing."

"And what's that?" Hannah demanded icily.

"Tch, tch, madam, if you haven't noticed you must be more ill than we think you are. I assure you, Miss Lucie hasn't missed anything. She's been in a state, I can tell you."

"About nothing," Hannah snapped. "She's an hysterical fool. She suffers from obsessive jealousy. Does she think her behaviour is calculated to keep her husband?"

"So you have noticed it, madam. But I warned you,

didn't I? You wanted this girl to be like Miss Dolly, and I said if she was you could expect trouble."

"Dolly, Dolly, Dolly!" Hannah hissed. "I'm sick of the very sound of her name."

"You're overtired, madam." Patterson's voice was concerned, cosy, reassuring. "That's all that it is. You need a good night's sleep. I'm going to give you some of the sleeping draught the doctor left. And in the morning I'll ask him to come and look you over. After that crazy trip—it's a wonder you're still alive. And it's Miss Juana's birthday. You want to be well for that."

"Sleep!" said Hannah irritably. "What nonsense. I'm going down to dinner." She allowed herself a macabre smile. "I can't wait to meet your brilliant nephew."

CHAPTER ELEVEN

DINNER, the only time of the day when they were all together.

Fabrice was saying querulously, "Do you mean to say you bought nothing at all, Mama? You had that long trip for nothing?"

"I told you—I wasn't well enough to get out to the palace. Patrick went. He said the collection was extraordinarily dull. A pity, but that's how it goes." Hannah had kept to her decision to come down to dinner. She looked devastatingly tired, but she sat stubbornly erect, her hair swept up to be held by one of her beautiful tortoiseshell combs, the long jade ear-rings swinging from her ears. It almost looked as if she had dressed up to impress Patterson's nephew, though he, as she had expected, failed to impress her. He was exactly as she had expected him to be, although he had outgrown the spots of adolescence. He was tall and slouched, his hair was too long and needed washing, and he had a sharp insensitive face. It wasn't true to say he didn't impress Hannah. He did, but for the wrong reasons.

"Anyway, Emily was able to visit her first Spanish palace, and that was important. Wasn't it, Emily?"

"I enjoyed it enormously," said Emily.

"I don't understand you, Mama. You're talking like a tourist. Charming as Emily is, we're not in business to show her round Spain." Fabrice looked at Emily apologetically. "I wish we were."

"This was a place I wanted Emily to see," Hannah said shortly. "Let's leave it at that. And tell me, Raymond," her lizard eyes rested on the young man at the end of the table, "are you planning to visit the other show places of Spain? You must go to Seville, of course, and I'd recommend the mosque at Cordoba, and the Escorial."

"I find Granada marvellous. Quite marvellous." The young man's only resemblance to his aunt was his stolidity, that could have been stupidity, except that Hannah knew well enough that it wasn't.

"I want to spend a lot of time in the Alhambra Palace, and I'd like to hear the nightingales sing in the Generalife Gardens. I understand this happens?" He questioned the table at large, but his eyes were on Emily. He believed in going straight towards his objective. It was quite clear that he would enjoy her company on his sight-seeing.

It was Lucie who became animated.

"Oh, yes, it happens. You ought to take Emily. She hasn't heard them yet. Wouldn't you like to hear them, Emily? It's terribly romantic there in the moonlight. Isn't it, darling?" Her gaze on Patrick was intimate and possessive. "Actually that's where my husband proposed to me. We often go there still, to the exact spot. Don't we, darling?"

"I'm sure Raymond isn't interested in your memoirs," Hannah said unsympathetically. "Let me talk to him. I want to know why he has decided so suddenly to give us the pleasure of a visit from him. It was sudden, wasn't it, Raymond?"

The young man's flat grey eyes were remarkably like Patterson's.

"I'd been planning it for a long time, Mrs. Romero. Hadn't my aunt told you?"

"To be sure she had. You're the apple of her eye. She's been looking forward to this for years. But I understood you were deep in your studies still."

"This is part of my studies, Mrs. Romero," Raymond said in his prim voice. "Travel to the sites of the old styles of architecture is extremely important. I shall find this trip particularly rewarding, I hope."

There was something a little repellent about the young man's precise plans for his future. Emily thought that the others felt it, too, for there was a little silence round the table.

Then Hannah said raucously, "Don't have dreams about building Moorish palaces in Surbiton, young man. You may, just possibly, come unstuck." She began to laugh. There was something forced about her rich chuckle. "To forgive a vulgar expression. But I think you know what I mean."

If the young man had the intelligence he implied he had, he would know exactly what she meant. His aunt had made a *faux pas*. In spite of enlightened times, Hannah had remained unenlightened. Patterson was a servant. A servant didn't introduce her relations as guests into her mistress's house. If Raymond wasn't aware of this, it must be pointed out to him.

But Raymond didn't appear to be thin-skinned. He went off to bed later, as if he had every right to occupy a room in the house. And Emily, listening and watching, knew that Patterson had sent for him to come to Granada. And that Cousin Hannah, beneath her intimidating courtesy, was angry and alarmed.

She resented this small problem taking her attention. She would have given deeper thought to it if she hadn't been so absorbed in what was happening to Patrick and Lucie. Were they having a reconciliation in their room tonight? Was Patrick telling Lucie about the possible visit to Paris? Or was she making him recapture the moment in the Generalife Gardens, when the ancient everlasting beauty of the avenues of cypresses, ink-black against the moon, the silvered jets of the fountains, the roses turned dark in the night light, had swept them into each others arms?

There had been a tormented look in Lucie's eyes that Emily was uneasily afraid nothing would banish.

If Patterson were aware of her *faux pas* she gave no sign of it. She suggested quite blatantly that it would be a nice idea if Emily were to show Raymond the sights.

"I don't know them myself," Emily said coldly.

"Then, there you are, the two of you can discover them together. I wouldn't be surprised if Raymond can't tell you a lot about things already. He reads everything up."

"I'm sure he does."

"Oh, yes," said Patterson, unaware of Emily's sarcasm. "In fact I was saying to the mistress, what a pity Raymond hadn't been with you at the *Palacio del Sol*. He'd have had its history at his fingertips. As it was, I don't suppose you even found out who that old Don Jaime was."

"No," said Emily coolly. "Who was he?"

Ever so slightly, Patterson floundered. "Don't ask me. I was only saying Raymond would have found out."

In spite of being slightly off balance, Patterson's words had a vague menace, as if she were telling Emily obliquely that Raymond was here to find out everything. She had satisfied herself that Emily knew nothing, and had noticed nothing, not even the portrait with its echo of Fabrice's dark melancholy. It was none of Emily's business, but it was the business of Raymond Patterson, abruptly summoned from his studies in London.

She wanted to tell Patrick this. Patrick, with his obscure talk of daggers and the necessity for being forewarned, knew, or suspected, something too. He had been more observant than she on that trip to Madrid.

She would have to wait until she could find him alone in his studio tomorrow. After Patterson's departure—her visit had been on the pretext of telling Emily that Hannah had settled down nicely in her own bed after the long exhausting day—it seemed as if everyone was in bed. The house was silent. But she herself was far from being sleepy. She stood at her open window listening to the now familiar trickle of the fountains, the sound of water that the Moors took with them wherever they went since they came from the desert where water was life. Stars were shining in the black velvet sky. There must have been a moon, too, for the opposite wall of the house shone in a washed eerie light. The maze was in dark shadow. But beyond it a light sprang on, shining in thin yellow lines through a shuttered window.

Emily's heart leaped. It was the window of Patrick's studio.

So he was there. He was not sharing the intimacy of Lucie's bedroom after all. Emily thought of it as entirely Lucie's since the day she had been called into it for something and noticed its ruffles and its femininity. It smelt of the sweet heavy perfume Lucie wore, and its shutters were always closed.

Now was her opportunity to talk to him alone. She hastily slipped off her nightgown and pulled a dress over her head.

She was putting her feet into soft-soled shoes when she stopped.

No. Valid as was her reason for talking to Patrick, she couldn't do this. He would be standing there painting with great slashes, his face tight, angry, secret, hollow with tiredness. He would either mock what she said, or he would kiss her. And if he kissed her it wouldn't be like it had been in the hotel in Cordoba. It would be a real kiss, passionate and painful, and they wouldn't know what to do afterwards because a bridge would have been irrevocably crossed.

Stay where you are, she told herself fiercely. Show that you do have commonsense after all.

It will come right, she whispered later, the tears on her cheeks. But how?

It was dawn before she slept, and the light still shone from Patrick's studio.

Emily wondered who else had slept last night. She was sure Hannah had been too overtired to rest. Lucie, one was almost certain, would have lain listening for Patrick's footsteps. Fabrice might have had a good night, although he had looked strangely careworn yesterday.

But one didn't expect Maria, the plump pretty maid, to have shadows beneath her eyes. However, it appeared that all Maria was worried about was a quarrel with her boy friend. She burst into tears when Emily questioned her, and snuffled noisily.

"Jose said I was bad-tempered, senorita. He said he wouldn't want such a bad-tempered wife. And he said I was liking to spend too much money." Maria's voice rose in a wail. "Just because I had a new blouse specially for him. He didn't even say it was pretty, he just said I spend too much money."

"He'll get over it, Maria. If that's all it is."

"All, senorita! Isn't it enough?"

Emily smiled wryly. "I think there could be a way round that problem, Maria. A kiss can do an awful lot. Why don't you meet Jose and kiss him?"

"With Mama and all my sisters watching?" Maria was shocked and tear-stained and very pretty. "You don't understand, senorita. I am never permitted to see Jose alone."

"Come, Maria! What are you made of? Be naughty. Be bold. Surely you can think of some way to see him alone."

Maria began to giggle.

"I admit to you, senorita, I have already done so, once or twice. I write him a little letter and say perhaps he would be passing somewhere at such a time. But after we are such bad friends, do you think he would listen to my letter?"

"I expect if he loves you he will. Anyway, it would be a way to find out." Emily was weary of the subject. She didn't want to start envying Maria her comparatively uncomplicated problem. "How is Juana today?"

"Oh, she is happy. It's her birthday. And her doll is finished. She is to have her gifts this morning when the old senora comes downstairs. Patterson says that will be just before lunch, because madam is very tetchy this morning and refuses to stay in bed." Maria clapped her hand to her mouth, aware of her indiscretion. But the laughter shone in her black eyes. "What is tetchy, senorita?"

"It's cross, *impaciente.*"

"I understand, senorita. It's what everyone is this morning. Me, too, with that Jose." Maria shrugged and made a sad face, but her unhappiness had gone. She had solved her problem. Lucky Maria.

It was impossible, however, not to catch Juana's excitement. The child was almost pretty, with a wild rose color in her usually colorless cheeks, and her eyes darkened with anticipation. Her thin fine pale hair had been fluffed out and she wore an immaculately starched white frock.

"I'm eight," she said to Emily. "Is that old?"

"Quite old, darling."

"Mummy says I don't need to have any lessons today because it's my birthday. And I mustn't cry because that's bad luck."

"What would you cry about on your birthday?"

"I hope I don't need to," Juana said seriously. "Mummy has, but it doesn't matter because it isn't her birthday."

Lucie showed no traces of tears when she came in, but she was very sallow and there were dark stains beneath her eyes. She looked plain, a thin plain sulky woman whose eyes didn't quite meet anybody's. Although when Patrick came in they flashed for a second with that disturbing tormented unbalanced look, and her hands on her lap clenched slowly until they looked like claws.

Watching, Emily had a moment of pure concern and apprehension. Lucie was becoming unreachable, she divined. No loving words of Patrick's were going to penetrate her stubbornly closed mind. She wanted to torment herself. It was the way she was made.

Fabrice sat by Emily, and presently Hannah came in, leaning heavily on her stick. She, too, bore marks of either the too exhausting trip she had made, or of a sleepless night. She looked ten years older and there was a grim look to her face that she couldn't, or didn't, try to conceal. It didn't promise to be a gay party that Juana was to have. Fortunately the child was too excited to be aware of the strangely brooding atmosphere. Patterson at least, who had been at every birthday anniversary in this house for nearly half a century, was placid and smiling, and Raymond (who had invited him? Emily wondered) wore an expression of mild interest and tolerance.

"My cake! Where's my cake?" Juana screamed.

"Pet, your manners," Lucie protested. "Which will you do first, unwrap your parcels or blow out your candles?"

"The candles first," Juana insisted. "Then I'm really eight."

Maria had come in, carrying the cake, and Juana excitedly pointed at the candles. She wanted to strike the matches to light them herself. Her loose hair hung over the flame and Hannah gasped in apprehension.

"Let her, Mama," said Lucie. "Anything for peace."

The frail flames bloomed, and then died in a quiver of blue smoke as Juana triumphantly blew them all out.

"Now I'm eight," she cried. "Now I can have my parcels."

Fabrice murmured to Emily, "I hope she likes the doll. She might think it a bit old-fashioned. But it has quite a modern face. I suppose people's faces don't change much."

"No, they don't. Patrick and I saw your face in the *Palacio del Sol* and that must have been painted a hundred years ago."

Fabrice leaned forward. "What do you mean—my face?"

"It wasn't yours, but it was awfully like it." Emily hesitated, startled by the look on his face. He was staring at her too intensely, his mouth pinched and suspicious. "Patrick said it was some ancestor of Don Jaime's," she said uneasily.

"You do look very Spanish, you know," she added. "And I find a great similarity in Spanish faces. I expect I won't when I'm more used to them. You're like your father, your mother says."

"Yes," said Fabrice, moving his fingers across his lips. "I believe I am."

"But look! Look, everybody!" Juana was screaming. "It's a

gorgeous doll. It's the biggest I've ever had. Look, she has a hat, and even a parasol. And gloves!"

Behind Emily, Maria giggled with gratification. It was Hannah who said in a strange taut voice, "Juana! Show me the doll. Bring it here."

Juana skipped across willingly. "Look, grandmama! She has yellow curls. And her dress is purple."

"Lavender," said Hannah. "Who dressed this doll?"

Maria sketched a curtsey.

"It was me, senora."

"And who supplied you with the materials, the style?"

"The style, senora?" Maria frowned, puzzled.

"The fashion, girl. These long skirts, this ridiculous Edwardian bustle."

Patterson said in her expressionless voice, "As to that, madam, Maria came to me for materials and I remembered that old ball gown of Miss Dolly's. It's been hanging away for so long and the silk was perfect. A pity not to make use of it, I thought. Maria's a clever needlewoman. She thought it would be nice to copy the style exactly. I remembered the style of hat, and the parasol Miss Dolly always used to carry. It quite took me back."

"Your memory isn't very accurate, Patterson. Since when was a parasol carried with a ball gown? Even I know that's wrong, I who never had the opportunity to attend garden parties or go to balls."

"You do not like it, senora?" Maria asked anxiously.

"It looks perfect to me," said Lucie. "An Edwardian doll. Very clever, Maria. Isn't it, Fabrice?"

"Yes, it suits the age of the doll which is approximately the beginning of this century," Fabrice answered abstractedly. "You must admit that, Mama."

"Oh, yes. I can remember, too," Hannah said in a dry, cracked voice. "I never knew you'd kept that gown, Patterson. You didn't tell me."

"It was her favorite, madam. The one she looked loveliest in. It even smells a little of her perfume still."

"Isn't this—a little macabre?" Lucie said, with a faint shiver. "Juana darling, do you really like your new doll? If you don't, I'm sure Uncle Fabrice—"

Juana clutched the waxen creature tightly to her small bosom.

"I love her, Mummy. I love her. Thank you very much, Uncle Fabrice."

"She curtseys," Fabrice said heavily. "I'll show you."

Juana watched absorbedly as he lifted the doll's lavender skirts and inserted the key in her back.

"What's macabre?" she asked.

"I think I will go to my room," said Hannah. "No, Patterson. Stay here and enjoy the fun. Emily will help me."

"Of course," Emily said, springing to her side, and wondering why there was that curious half smile on Raymond's face.

The party, although fortunately Juana didn't realize it, had been ruined. No one but Raymond the interloper seemed to find that fact amusing.

Anything for peace, Lucie had said. But there was to be no peace in that house.

Late in the afternoon the place was rent by Juana's screams. She had come rushing in from outdoors, her face scarlet, her white party frock limp against her perspiring body.

It was a long time before anyone could understand what she said beyond the two words, "La Loca!"

Lucie had her in her arms immediately, soothing her and trying to make her talk coherently.

"But didn't Maria take you for a walk? Where is Maria?"

"La Loca took my doll! She took my new doll!"

It was true that Juana had taken the doll with her on her walk, but she was empty-handed now.

"What are you saying, honey? How could La Loca take your doll?"

"She did! She was hiding behind the gate and when I stopped she snatched it from me. Then she ran away. She was laughing."

"Honey, is this *true?* But there isn't any La Loca!"

Patrick knelt to take the trembling child from Lucie. "Let me talk to her. We must get this straight. Now, Juana. First of all, where was Maria when this happened?"

"She wasn't there. She was with Jose. She wasn't taking any notice of me, so I went down that street." Juana's eyes widened with distress. "I only wanted to peep in the gate, Daddy. Truly I did."

"That empty-headed Maria!" said Lucie, her face darkening. "Her mind is on nothing but her boy friends. She'll have to go, Patrick. If she can't be trusted to take Juana on a walk—"

"Wait a minute, Lucie. Let's hear Juana's story. Now, pet. You went to look in La Loca's gate, something frightened you and you dropped your doll and ran away."

"No, no, Daddy, I told you!" Juana was pummelling Patrick with her fists. "La Loca took my doll. Her hand came and snatched it."

"It was the old woman called Pilar, wasn't it? I expect she was only wanting to admire the doll."

"It wasn't Pilar. Pilar has black hair."

"And—this one—" Lucie's voice sounded frightened.

"It was white and tumbling down. I could hardly see her face. She was laughing. She ran away. It wasn't Pilar, Daddy. I talk to Pilar sometimes."

"Patrick, you'll have to go and see. Perhaps there is someone. Those stories—they could be true. I expect there are plenty of husbands who would like to shut their wives away." Her huge dilated eyes were on Patrick accusingly. "It's time someone got to the bottom of this."

"I agree. But one can't go bursting into a stranger's house."

"Then get the police."

"What! On a child's story? No, I'll find out for myself."

"Let me come with you," said Emily compulsively. The strange house in the Calle de Fatima was beginning to haunt her as it did Juana. This was obviously no gargoyle that Juana had imagined into a woman's face. It was a live creature, wild, lost.

Before Lucie could object, as no doubt in a calmer moment she would, Maria came bursting in, hot and distraught. Her relief, when she saw Juana, was overwhelming.

"Ah, thank God, there's the *nina*. She disappeared. I stopped for one moment only to speak to Jose; he happened to be sitting at a café just as we passed, wasn't it strange? I couldn't not stop to speak, could I, senora? One has to speak to one's future husband. And in that short moment" —she flung up her hands expressively—"Miss Juana had gone. Jose and I searched down every street. Then I came home to see if she had come by herself. And here, thank God, she is!"

"I lost my doll," Juana accused. But she was calmer now, her hysterics over. "It was your fault, Maria. I was bored with you talking to Jose. So I went to see La Loca."

Maria's hand flew to her mouth. "La Loca!" she breathed.

"Stay with your mother," Patrick said to Juana. He looked at Emily. "If you're coming, come."

CHAPTER TWELVE

THE house was not going to give up any of its secrets. Pilar, the chatelaine, grim-faced, a black scarf round her head, was seeing to that.

She answered Patrick's questions in emphatic Spanish, all the time shaking her head decisively. When Patrick, after pleading eloquently with her in her own language, made a move to go into the house Pilar flung her arms across the doorway, shouting, "No, no, no!" and adding something about the *"policia"*.

Emily could see nothing through the half open door but a tiled floor and bare white-washed walls. Someone moved in the shadows, and her heart leaped terrifyingly, but it was an elderly man, Pablo, Pilar's husband.

There were crickets whirring ceaselessly in the late afternoon heat. That sound, and the noise of fast traffic from the street, and Pilar's vociferous voice made it impossible to be sure whether there was a faint high singing from somewhere in the house. A moment later the heavy door slammed unceremoniously in hers and Patrick's face.

Patrick looked angry and baffled. He stepped back to look up at the closed shutters of the upstairs room. Even the one that had been a little ajar the other day was now closed.

"What did she say?" Emily asked. "I couldn't understand."

"I suppose exactly what one would expect—if she is being paid to keep silent."

"About—someone hidden?"

"Who knows? Methinks she doth protest too much! But what can we do? She threatened to send her husband for the police if we came in uninvited. She knows nothing about a doll. She had the nerve to say that if my daughter had lost a valuable doll she ought to be punished. I must say if there's someone there—"

"Yes?" said Emily breathlessly.

"She can't be having much fun with a jailer like that."

"I thought I heard someone singing. I couldn't be sure."

Patrick squinted upwards. He made an exasperated gesture.

"I suppose we can police the place ourselves, if we're determined to find out. But if someone wants to shut up a loony relative, it really isn't our business. Juana's been told to keep away from here. It's her own fault she's lost her doll. All the same—"

"It is something to do with us. You think that, don't you?"

Patrick took her arm, his fingers curving gently round her bare skin.

"Not with you, Emily. Not with you."

"Then the *Casa de Flor*. And that is me."

The flash of gentleness in his face was replaced by grimness.

"If anything in this house had to do with the *Casa de Flor* I'd have unearthed it long ago."

"But you didn't suspect it until a day or so ago, did you? When you said that to be forewarned was to be forearmed. What made you say that? What had you found out?"

"Not as much as I will," said Patrick. "Let's go."

Just outside the gate, loitering deliberately, was Patterson's nephew, Raymond.

"Hey, what did you find out?" he asked. His narrow face was inquisitive and avid. He wasn't there by chance. He was already making the *Casa de Flor*'s affairs his own. How dare he, Emily thought, and was delighted when Patrick answered:

"Only a dead body. The head rolled off when we touched it. It's an old Arab trick. If you don't care for blood"— Raymond had involuntarily gasped—"why don't you go and study the Alhambra Palace? It's much more in your line.

"Let him meddle in someone else's business," he muttered angrily as he took Emily away.

"He's rather a horror, isn't he?" Emily agreed. "How can silly old Patterson be so besotted about him?"

"Perhaps she won't be by the time he's gone," Patrick

answered, and sounded as if he were stating, not a prediction, but a fact.

Hannah was asleep, Patterson said. For the first time, Patterson's aplomb seemed a little shaken. Either because her practical joke (had it been a joke?) with the dressing of Juana's doll hadn't come off, or because the subsequent development had shaken her. She hadn't even the expected prosaic explanation that Juana was a picturesque little liar. She merely said in a hushed voice, "Madam needs the rest. I wouldn't like her disturbed."

"I won't disturb her," said Emily. "I'm just going to sit beside her."

"I don't think—"

"Because I want to," Emily said shortly.

She didn't add that she wanted to be the one to tell Hannah of this new development, and to do it gently. Hannah had already suffered enough of a shock from Patterson's morbid whim to have the doll dressed as a replica of Dolly. Something very odd was going on. And Hannah was either at the heart of it, or she was as much mystified and disturbed as everyone else.

She lay very quietly, her breath making scarcely a sound. She was surrounded by the treasures gathered during her life; the exquisite lace bedspread and the ornate antique bed, the beautiful old mirror and furniture, the fine rugs. She looked to be a rich and pampered old woman. Yet even in sleep her face had a careworn look, as if she were sunk deep in a tortuous dream.

This was obviously so, for suddenly her hands on the coverlet twitched, her mouth began to work. Suddenly her eyes sprang open.

"She's trying to steal my ring!" she gasped thickly.

Emily sprang up to bend over her.

"Who is, Cousin Hannah?"

In the way of someone talking in her sleep, Hannah answered quite logically, "Dolly! She's taking my ring!"

She threshed in the bed, struggling with an unseen adversary, her face contorted, her unseeing eyes fixed accusingly on Emily.

Patterson was there, moving on silent feet.

"She's having one of her nightmares." She raised her voice briskly, "Wake up, madam! You're dreaming. This isn't Miss Dolly, it's Miss Emily. She doesn't want your ring."

The familiar voice penetrated Hannah's sleep-drugged consciousness. Slowly comprehension came back to her eyes. She was very pale and bathed in perspiration.

"I'm not mad! I was only dreaming." Her eyes sought Patterson's—there was appeal, and a dreadful uncertainty in her face. "I thought Dolly was taking my ring. This aquamarine. It used to be hers. I thought she'd come back for it."

"Is she likely to?" Emily couldn't help saying the words. They seemed to be forced out of her.

The two old women, the one in the bed and the other solid as a rock beside it, stared at her.

"Good gracious, Emily, it's I who was dreaming," Hannah said at last.

For the first time her voice was unfriendly.

"In any case, what are you doing here watching over me? I'm not ill." She seemed to imply that Emily was eavesdropping. "And why was Juana screaming a little while ago? I thought she had promised not to cry on her birthday."

"She was crying because she has lost her doll," Emily said.

Hannah started up.

"Impossible! How?"

"She's put it down somewhere in the street and forgotten it," Patterson said evenly. "You know how careless she is. I've sent Raymond out to look for it."

"Is that what he's doing?" Emily said sceptically. "He seemed to be hanging about La Loca's house."

"La Loca!" Hannah exclaimed. "Emily—have you been listening to that ridiculous story, too?"

"Juana said an old woman with white hair snatched her new doll and ran inside," Emily said evenly. "Patrick and I went to the house to investigate."

Hannah's eyes had lost their lethargy. They were hooded, like a lizard's, the topaz pupils gleaming.

"And what did you discover?"

"A very unpleasant woman called Pilar who threatened to call the police. We decided she was so aggressive because she had something to hide."

"And that would be her own business, I imagine. You can't go about demanding to know the secrets of strangers."

"And what about the doll?"

"Juana has an inventive imagination."

"But if you'd seen her, Cousin Hannah. She was terrified."

Patterson moved calmly about the room, laying out Hannah's clothes for the evening.

"Naturally. She wanted a good excuse for losing that expensive new doll. As madam says, Miss Emily, she's a fair terror at making things up. But wait till Raymond gets home."

Patterson seemed to have some private knowledge that Raymond would return with the doll—as he did. He flung it on the table saying casually, "Left it on a seat in the gardens. I found some kids playing with it. It's got a bit grubby." He looked very pleased with himself, as if he had accomplished a fine piece of detection work. "That kid can make up stories, can't she? Has she always been like that?"

Lucie said coldly, "Juana always speaks the truth," but she looked puzzled, all the same. She examined the doll, her fingers exploring the tear in the lavender silk dress. "Maria will have to dress it again," she said absently.

Patrick was looking at Raymond thoughtfully. He didn't say what he was thinking. He merely observed, to Lucie, "I think you're right about Maria, darling. She can't be trusted while she's in this lovesick state. She ought to have noticed the doll was left behind."

For some reason his quiet voice provoked Lucie to violent anger.

"Are you saying that Juana tells lies?" she demanded, her face twisted. "Are you taking their side against me? But I might have known you would!"

"Lucie—"

"If you're prepared to believe this—" She looked at Raymond with acute dislike—"this complete stranger rather than your own daughter, then I can see how much you care for us!"

It was the first time Lucie had quarrelled with Patrick in the presence of other people. Emily wanted to cry out at the pain and distaste on Patrick's face. It was as if Lucie had lost all pride since Patrick's return from Toledo. She was not going to keep her unhappiness private any longer.

And was the episode of the lost doll over?

It seemed to be, but Emily couldn't believe it was. For one thing, Juana refused to touch it. She shrank from it, saying it was dirty. And another thing had happened. Packers had come to the house to pack the lovely white and gold

Meissen dinner service. Fabrice had a buyer waiting for it. The price offered had been too good to refuse. So that was two of Hannah's adored treasures, the Louis the Fifteenth clock and the Meissen set, to go. And Hannah didn't say a word.

There was plenty left, of course. But Emily had a feeling that within weeks the house would be stripped, that a queer rot had set in and couldn't be stopped.

Juana's birthday proved to have been a strange and melancholy day for everyone. Except perhaps for Raymond who said he had had a fabulous time exploring the city.

Immediately after dinner Lucie said that she was going to bed. She had a bad headache and intended to take some pills.

Patrick went up to her a little later. Emily found the thought of sleep impossible. She wandered into the courtyard, trying to think of nothing but the balmy night air, the cool tinkle of water and the scent of jasmine. Presently Fabrice came out to smoke a cigarette before going to bed. But he was even more silent than usual, and didn't say a word for quite ten minutes, standing puffing at his cigarette, a solid gloomy figure, his head sunk on his chest.

Emily wondered what he was worrying about: the episode of Juana's doll, or the sale of the Meissen dinner service.

Finally Emily asked him which story he believed about the missing doll, Juana's or Raymond's.

With some asperity he told her not to bother her head about things that didn't concern her, then almost at once he apologized, looking ashamed.

"I'm sorry, Emily, I've had rather a day of it. I have an awkward decision to make. I'm not good at decisions. I'm not good at much at all." He was mumbling, his head sunk down again.

Emily felt sorry for him, without knowing why.

"You're terribly good at your clocks and things."

"Yes, that's all I really want to be. A clockmaker. Clocks are nice untroublesome things. Well—I'll say good-night. You ought to get some sleep, too."

Emily said Yes, but still lingered in the fragrant night air, and knew why she had lingered when Patrick came out. It might seem that she had been waiting for him, although that thought hadn't come into her consciousness until now.

"Why aren't you in bed, Emily?"

"Why aren't you? You didn't sleep last night, either."

He looked at her sharply.

"I saw your light in the studio. Do you work well when you work such long hours?"

He flung down the match he had struck to light his cigarette.

"You know damn well I don't." He added, "You know too much."

"Too much and not enough. What *is* wrong with Lucie? It can't just be jealousy of you and me. She couldn't have got as bad as this just since my arrival. She looks unbalanced."

"She's on the verge of a breakdown, I think," Patrick said tiredly. "No, it isn't just you, Emily. You've only been one more stick on a fire that was lighted—oh, before we were married. I suppose I was flattered then when she couldn't bear me to look at any other woman. I didn't know what that sort of nature would be like to live with. Lucie is chronically unhappy, chronically everything, suspicious, mistrusting, insecure. I don't know who or what's done it to her; Hannah, I suppose. Hannah's a great many wonderful things, but maternity doesn't shine among them. Oh, Lucie wasn't this bad at first. She tried. She's so bewildered and mixed-up. I tried, too. I shouldn't be talking to you like this."

"Patrick!" Emily could say no more than his name.

"I've been flippant and facetious with you. I tried to believe I was hiding my feelings. I don't suppose I deceived you."

She shook her head. "If you had, I'd have wanted to kill you."

His eyes glinted with brief amusement.

"What a very direct person you are."

"Never mind what I am. What are we to *do?*"

"Stop waiting. Stop being decent. Stop trying to do the impossible. It's time, Emily," he said very soberly. "It really is time. It's our turn to be happy. The way we were that day in Toledo. It was happiness for you, wasn't it?"

"Oh, yes. Oh, yes," she whispered.

"I haven't been in Lucie's bed for three years. It's another thing she's come to hate. Has always hated, I suspect. I have to tell you this because I love you."

He didn't attempt to touch her. He was clinging to an iron self-control that she guessed he had exercised for years. Her own was less strong. She knew that in a moment she would be in his arms even though every window of the *Casa de Flor* had its avid witness.

"We can go away," he went on. "But there's Juana. How can we leave Juana with a mother like that? Do you see now the truth of what I told you when you arrived?"

"Yes, I do. And you were right to be angry with me for coming. I have only aggravated the situation. Oh, Patrick." She was beginning to tremble. "It's a queer house. We don't belong here, either of us. But we can't abandon Juana. And Hannah—"

"Hannah is an old woman who's reaping the whirlwind."

Emily drew back, laughing uneasily. "If you're going to talk like a Biblical prophet! What do you mean?"

"Who sows the wind reaps the whirlwind. Hannah's been a deliberate and dedicated sower."

"What are you talking about? Patterson's tyranny? She is a tyrant, you know. A tyrant in soft shoes, sneaking. But I suppose that's inevitable after so many years together."

"I mean much more than that," Patrick said grimly. "Apart from Patterson, Hannah has ruined Fabrice and Lucie, simply with her dominating personality and her fixed ideas. She may have done it unconsciously, but that doesn't make her deserve sympathy, although she has a way of getting round your affections, the old devil. She's a very powerful woman and I should think she's had her own way all her life."

"Not while she was young!" Emily protested. "She had nothing. She had to take orders from other people."

"Can you imagine her doing that?"

"No, I can't. But she must have had to, in a compromising sort of way, until there was some opportunity to seize."

"Exactly."

"Do you mean coming to Spain after Dolly was the opportunity she was waiting for?"

"She turned it to her own advantage, didn't she?" Patrick said evasively.

"I know she met Ferdie and married. What are you trying to tell me?"

"I think the old girl's had a change of heart. She's taken a good look at herself and not much liked what she's seen. People do that when they're suffering from a mortal illness. Why do you imagine she sent for you."

"Because I remind her of Dolly," Emily answered promptly.

"Oh—you think she did Dolly some wrong. That was the opportunity she seized when she came to Spain."

Patrick said, "I'm certain of it." He looked disturbed and unhappy. "I'm fond of Hannah. I dislike dipping into other people's secrets. They're their own property, and private. But I think there's no alternative."

"Something about that house in the Calle de Fatima?" Emily had a queer feeling of dread. "It was the thing you found out in Madrid."

"The beginning of it. I must know who the owner of that house is. I couldn't find out today because the land offices had shut. But first thing in the morning—"

"What will you do first thing in the morning?" came Raymond's drawling voice behind them.

How long had he been there? He wore soft shoes, like his aunt. He might have heard their entire conversation.

Patrick gave him a long, level look.

"You do have a habit of popping up, don't you? It must be a family characteristic."

Raymond had the grace to look a little flustered.

"I only came out for a little air."

"Then stay and enjoy it," Patrick said largely. "Emily, it's time you went up. I'm just going to finish a small job in the studio. We'll talk again tomorrow. In the morning. Come to my studio about eleven o'clock. I'll be back by then."

"Back from where?" Ignoring her question, and ignoring Raymond too, he bent his head and kissed her, his lips brushing hers at first, and then, for the briefest moment, pressing hard, hurting. As if he couldn't help himself, and didn't care any longer who saw.

He tilted her chin gently. "Hold that up. There'll be a way."

And after that he expected her to sleep.

She walked about her room, and every time the tears dried in her cheeks, more flowed to wet them all over again.

What were they to do? Lucie, Juana, Hannah . . . None of these people could be abandoned. What was there they could do? Where would they find a way?

CHAPTER THIRTEEN

EMILY didn't think she had been asleep for more than a few minutes before she heard the scream.

Juana, she thought, then knew at once it hadn't been a child's scream. It had been long drawn out, mortally afraid.

Almost at once the house was full of footsteps. Patterson was running down the passage past Emily's door in the direction of Lucie's room.

"Miss Lucie!" she gasped. She had already identified the voice.

But Lucie's room was empty, the bed rumpled, the windows and shutters wide open and the night air flowing in.

Where was she? Had she, too, rushed out to see who had screamed?

"I could swear it was her!" Patterson said, looking round in bewilderment.

Hannah had come limping to the door in her nightgown. In her hurry she had neither stopped to put on a wrap nor to pin up her hair. With her untidy grey locks and distraught face she must look like La Loca, Emily thought involuntarily, the old woman who wasn't supposed to exist. Behind her was Raymond, who had come leaping up the stairs. He was still fully dressed. He must have just come in from enjoying the night air.

"I heard a God-awful scream," he said breathlessly. "Who was it?"

"Juana hasn't woken up, thank goodness," said Patterson. "I looked in there. It must have been Miss Lucie. But where is she?"

Hannah had limped slowly to the open window, leaning on her stick. She stood in the fresh air, her thin nightgown outlined about her scrawny body. She seemed to sway and Emily hurried to her side.

The window looked out over the maze. Emily knew that the apprehension seizing her at that moment had also seized

Hannah. The windows reached to the floor and beyond them was a narrow balcony with a low railing. Even sober, one had only to lean incautiously over the railing to take a tumble. But supposing one had been unsteady with sleeping pills. . . .

Before Emily had accustomed her eyes to the darkness outside she saw the movement among the clipped privet hedges. And the glimmer of some pale garment caught.

Then she heard Patrick's voice. "Get help! Quickly!"

It was Patterson who flew to the telephone to get a doctor. Emily was fully occupied in supporting Hannah who had collapsed into her arms. Fabrice helped Patrick carry Lucie inside. Raymond had turned the colour of pale cheese and muttered that he couldn't stand the sight of blood.

But there wasn't much blood. It hadn't been a long fall, and Lucie's face was only scratched a little with the sharp twigs of the privet. She didn't seem to have any broken bones, although Patrick was afraid to examine her too closely before the doctor arrived. She was unconscious.

Hannah refused to go back to bed. Although she had collapsed she hadn't lost consciousness, and she insisted on being propped in a chair near Lucie.

"Why did she do it?" she kept saying.

"Do it?" said Patrick in his grim voice. "You hardly think she jumped deliberately!"

"How could she fall? How could she just fall?"

The awful thing was that Hannah seemed to expect Lucie's fall to be something much more sinister than an accident. As if nothing so simple as accidents happened in this house.

"If I may make a suggestion," said Patterson, who had recovered from her initial panic and was now her usual calm and capable self, "Miss Lucie used to get into a state whenever she heard the servants giggling in the maze. You know how they are always doing that, madam, in spite of orders. I expect she'd heard them tonight, and went to the window to reprimand them. She was probably dizzy from the pills she had taken for her headache. You heard her say she was going to take some."

"That does sound a probable explanation," said Fabrice worriedly. "Lucie did have a down on courting couples. Said it was vulgar."

Emily saw the tightness of Patrick's face. He held one of Lucie's hands in his. Even now he was trying to reach her. Poor Lucie, who both wanted and hated love.

Without looking up, he said, "There's no need to make guesses. Lucie will tell us herself what happened."

"If she can," said Hannah starkly.

At first the doctor talked of moving her to hospital. If the unconsciousness persisted, there might be the possibility of a skull fracture. But he thought it was only a little concussion, and Lucie would most likely recover consciousness shortly.

Hannah's and Patterson's eyes met in a long look.

"She's not to go to the hospital," Hannah said definitely. "Patterson will nurse her here. Patterson is a skilled nurse."

"But, madame—"

"My cousin Dolly died through my folly in trying to move her to hospital," said Hannah harshly. "I never forgave myself. I won't risk the same thing happening to Lucie. I want her to stay here."

Patrick took the doctor aside.

"Is it important to move her tonight?"

"Perhaps not. The level of unconsciousness seems light. It's very likely she'll come to with nothing more than a bad headache."

"Patrick!" cried Hannah. "I won't let her out of my sight. She may be your wife, but she's my daughter, and I insist."

The doctor shrugged. "In that case! Otherwise I can see I will have two patients. Keep her still. If she shows any sign of becoming worse I will come immediately. But I predict she will be sitting up in the morning asking what has happened. But you, madame," he turned to Hannah, "I won't be answerable for you if you disobey me any more. I order you to bed at once."

Hannah lifted her ravaged face.

"Doctor! When my daughter recovers, will her brain be all right?"

"She may have a little loss of memory. Nothing more, with luck."

Hannah relaxed. "Thank God!" she murmured. *La Loca*, Emily thought with a shiver, reading Hannah's thoughts.

Shortly after the doctor had left Lucie did recover consciousness. But she didn't remember a thing that had happened. She said she had a bad headache and asked why

Patterson was sitting by her bed. When she saw her scratched face she cried out in horror, but still had no memory of leaning over the balcony to look into the dark maze.

"If I heard the servants," she said distastefully, "I would close the window."

Anyway, Maria swore that none of them had been in the maze. Concita had had the evening off to go and visit her family, and Maria had been ironing in the kitchen while Sebastian cleaned the silver. They had seen and heard nothing.

It was Patrick who had found Lucie, as if he had known just where to look. He said he had heard her cry from his studio. Emily couldn't help noticing the sideways glances that Maria and Concita gave him at breakfast. They thought he and Lucie had quarrelled again. They knew his quick temper. Perhaps, in a flash of rage, he had helped his wife to fall. . . .

Raymond thought the same. He kept giving Patrick looks beneath his thick pale lashes. Raymond had seen Patrick kiss Emily in the courtyard. He had, of course, told his aunt. That was why Patterson had refused to leave Lucie's bedside, and still sat there, even neglecting her usually devoted care of Hannah. Hannah didn't know what to think. But she was afraid. Emily had seen the flash of intense relief in her eyes when she heard that Lucie had recovered, then the fear.

Fabrice was silent, and it was impossible to guess his thoughts. He only looked as if he hadn't slept for a long time, his melancholy eyes bloodshot and sunken, so that he had a vague and disturbing look of someone about to face the inquisition. Indeed, he had scarcely spoken a word in Emily's hearing since she had told him about the portrait in the *Palacio del Sol*. Supposing Hannah had committed an infidelity, supposing Fabrice were not, after all, Ferdie's son. Would it need to bother him so much?

But Emily hadn't time to worry about Fabrice wrestling with his personal problems. She was too occupied with being furious that anyone should suspect Patrick, and also too busy reassuring Juana.

Juana was shocked to find her mother in bed and for once not at her beck and call. Her face went very white when she was told and her mind immediately flew to disaster. "Is she going to die?"

"Of course she isn't," said Emily. "She's only resting. She's very tired."

"Why is she very tired?"

"Because she hasn't been sleeping well lately. The doctor says she must rest."

Juana clutched Emily's hands.

"Why did the doctor come? Mummy *is* going to die."

"Silly baby, I told you she isn't. Why don't you go in the garden and pick her some flowers? Patterson will let you give them to her, I'm sure. After that, it will be time for your music lesson."

"Am I to have a lesson while Mummy's sick?"

"Of course. Don't you think it's time we had a look to see how the handkerchief doll is? She's been shut in the piano for a long time."

Juana debated, her eyes less alarmed.

"What kind of flowers?" she asked in her intense voice.

"Some jasmine. A rose. Don't be so helpless. Go and find them yourself. But put on your hat. The sun's hot."

Juana began to go towards the door, trailing her straw hat. Suddenly she turned back and subjected Emily to her fierce blue gaze.

"If Mummy dies, will *you* look after me?"

"Juana! What a question! Mummy isn't going to die. Don't say that again."

Indeed, why should Lucie die? She had a slight concussion, a perhaps convenient loss of memory. And there was fear in Hannah's eyes. . . .

Before Juana came back with her posy of flowers there was another unexpected happening. Raymond was leaving.

He came clattering down the stairs, carrying his bag. Patterson was standing at the top of the stairs calling something to him, something that sounded like "Coward!"

Raymond called back over his shoulder, "I've changed my mind, that's all."

Then he saw Emily and gave a weak grin. "Are you running away from something?" she asked. She hadn't expected the color to flood his face as it did.

"I've only decided to move on. Granada was only part of my itinerary."

"What a sudden young man you are. Arriving out of the blue, and leaving so soon. I thought you were going to show me the sights."

"You say that now, when there's no danger of me asking

you," he said waspishly. He gave her an impertinent stare. "I'd thought you were otherwise occupied. Especially now." He was referring to Lucie being confined to her bed and Patrick being free. Emily wanted to slap his sly pale face. "Anyway, I'm moving on. I've seen all I want to here." He looked up at Patterson hovering at the top of the stairs. "Thank the old lady for me. I'll send you an address later for writing to me. I'll probably be in Rome."

"Quite a grand tour," Emily said.

He was thin-skinned, after all. He instantly said defensively, "It's part of my education. I'm not just throwing money away."

"I don't suppose you are, but I suspect you can thank your aunt for what you have."

Emily had no fondness for Patterson, but she suddenly felt sorry for the stout woman lingering at the top of the stairs. She must surely have found her nephew to be a great disappointment. The wretched Raymond had a callous look, as if he hadn't even bothered to thank her.

Raymond gave Emily a furtive look, muttering, "What business is it of yours? I must be off or I'll miss my train. Goodbye." He was gone, clattering over the tiled floor and out into the courtyard.

"He doesn't like accidents," Patterson said from the stairs. "He's sensitive."

"Is that why you called him a coward?"

"A coward! Raymond! Don't talk nonsense!" But Patterson's voice lacked conviction.

"Could you stay with Miss Lucie for a while?" she asked, coming down the stairs. "I have to go out for the mistress, and she doesn't want to be alone."

Patterson's voice had certainly lacked its customary vitality, but her appearance shocked Emily. She looked grey. The rosy plumpness of her face had gone. It had shrunken, and her eyes stared out of the lumpy flesh in a strange baleful way. Had Hannah been taunting her about Raymond? Or had Raymond's complete selfishness hurt her more than one had believed she could be hurt? Or was she just exhausted after her night up with Lucie? After all, she was seventy years old.

But that made another who looked frightened—Hannah, Fabrice, Raymond, Patterson . . .

And Lucie was the fifth. Lying on her luxurious pillows she looked scared to death.

Her enormous eyes sought Emily's.

"Where's Juana?"

"She's picking you some flowers. She'll be in in a moment, if you can stand her."

"Stand my own child!" Lucie said in her weak but still imperious voice. "I thought she would have been more upset that I was ill."

"She is very upset."

"Not the way she usually is. I don't believe she'd care much if I died. You'd comfort her."

"Oh, Lucie! Am I to spend the morning telling people you're not going to die?"

"Who wants to know?" Lucie was painfully interested.

"Well, Hannah. And then Juana. And I believe that ghastly nephew of Patterson's has gone off because he's scared of illness, or something. How do you feel, anyway?"

"Terrible," Lucie said faintly. "My head feels as if it will burst. And I can't think. I can't think!" she repeated in a panicky voice.

"Why do you have to think?" Emily wrung out a cloth in the wash basin, and gently placed it across Lucie's forehead. It was true that Lucie looked ill, her skin colorless, the bones shaped much too clearly beneath the flesh.

"Emily—" She clutched at Emily's hand, gripping it with disturbingly hot ones. "How did I fall? Did—" A look of agony came into her eyes—"did Patrick push me?"

"*Patrick?* Oh, Lucie!"

"I know you'd defend him. But how else did I fall? Who else would come in this room? If only I could remember!" She lay brooding. "I don't think I want to remember. Patterson says it will do no good. She says to forget it. But how can I go on not knowing? Patrick has never really loved me. Oh, he seemed to at first, but it didn't last. I could tell when it stopped. And since then he's tried to deceive me, and I've hated him for thinking me so stupid as to be deceived. Hated him. . . ." The shine in her eyes was really tears now. They were beginning to spill on to her cheeks. "Mama always told me never to risk loving anyone. It wasn't safe, she said, because they would hurt you or leave you or humiliate you. She never loved my father. Don't be fooled by the flowers on his grave act. She only married him to spite Dolly who she was so jealous of. She'd be married first, no matter what!"

"But I thought she was devoted to Dolly."

"Devoted!" echoed Lucie, with a short laugh. She was looking alarmingly tired. "No one's emotions in this house are what they seem. Haven't you found that out?"

"You ought to stop talking," Emily said uneasily.

But Lucie, on the verge of hysteria, could not stop. If she stopped, perhaps she would begin to brood again on how she had come to fall. Why had she been at the window? She had been dressed in nothing but a flimsy nightgown. She should have been in bed.

But what she had said explained a great deal.

Hannah's strange obsession about Dolly had been a black stain right through her life, and had spread to her children. Fabrice had turned inwards and become a solitary, trusting the heartbeat of a clock rather than a human being. And Lucie, emotionally starved and suspicious, had been unable to make a successful marriage.

Could all this have been because long ago one girl had been beautiful and adored, the other plain, unpopular, poor? No, there was much more to it than that. It must have been the circumstances surrounding Dolly's death. Hannah blamed herself for it. She had carried the guilt all these years, and then, in her old age, was trying to transfer her suppressed love for Dolly to Emily, trying vicariously to make amends. But amends for what?

"Where's Patrick?" Lucie asked, rolling her head restlessly. "Why doesn't he come near me? Is it because he's guilty?"

"Lucie! He sat and held your hand all the time you were unconscious."

"Did he?" Lucie's voice was full of longing. Then the old suspicions tightened her face again. "But he'd have to, to make himself look innocent. Why isn't he here now, when I can talk to him?"

"He had some urgent business." (What was he finding out about that house in the Calle de Fatima?) "He didn't go until he knew you were better. He'll be back soon."

"But I'm not better. My head feels terrible. Emily, *who* pushed me?"

"No one. You just fell. You'd taken sleeping pills, don't you remember?"

"But why was I at the window? There's something I can't quite remember. It's there—it just won't come. I had to go to the window. . . . *Why* did I go to the window?"

"Mummy! Mummy, I brought you some flowers," cried Juana, bursting into the room. She pushed the untidy bunch of brightly-coloured flowers at her mother. "Mummy, are you better?"

"Just a little, darling," Lucie said faintly.

"You're not going to die, are you, Mummy? Are you?"

Juana had flung her thin arms round Lucie. Lucie, in an endeavor to return the child's embrace, had gone a disturbing bluish color. Emily drew Juana away, telling her to put the flowers in water. "Ask Maria to give you a bowl."

"Oh yes. And I'll arrange them beautifully."

She flew off, her blonde pigtails bouncing.

"You see," said Lucie bitterly. "Already she doesn't care. You're taking her from me, Emily."

"I'm not at all," Emily denied indignantly. "But don't you want to see her looking well and happy?"

"And you think you can do that for her? Just as you can do it for my husband? Oh, I'm not blind!"

"Now, Lucie! What are you accusing Emily of?"

That was Hannah's voice. Hannah was coming very slowly into the room, as if she had little strength this morning. She had managed to put on her heavy silk dressing gown, but pinning up her hair had obviously been beyond her. The grey locks hung in disorder round her long yellow face. She was the shadow of Hannah the Governess, the plain, the unloved.

"Emily is taking everything from me, Mama! It's no use your saying she isn't." Lucie's voice was wild and accusing. "There she stands looking beautiful and innocent, but she isn't innocent at all, she's crafty and cunning and greedy, and she intends to have Patrick and Juana, everything!"

"You must be mad!" Emily whispered. "You must be mad!"

Hannah groped for a chair. For a minute it looked as if she would fall. She was having difficulty in breathing. When she did speak the words seemed to be forced from her.

"It couldn't happen again! Oh, what a dreadful thing!"

"What couldn't happen again?" Emily urged her. "Cousin Hannah! What are you talking about?"

She might have known that Hannah would not be out of control of herself for long. In a few moments she was able to look at Emily with composure although her eyes were infinitely crafty.

"Dolly once made the accusation that I was taking everything from her, her husband, her child. But she was out of her wits. With delirium," she added belatedly.

The darkened room, the two faces, Lucie's wild pallid one and Hannah's, secretive, cunning, full of its strange power, the heavy scent of the jasmine Juana had picked, the close heat, made Emily feel she was on the edge of a nightmare. She had to hear what Hannah was going to say, yet at the same time she wanted to run away from the knowledge.

"Poor Dolly's heart was broken over that scoundrel who deserted her. Her illness gave her the delusion that Ferdie was her husband and the baby we were expecting hers. It was so strange to have Dolly jealous of me." Hannah paused a moment, then said briskly, "That's why I said Lucie was foolishly doing the same thing. Emily will find her own husband, Lucie. She's independent and strong, not like Dolly who was brought up to lean on people. But we're all upset today, even silly old Patterson over that worthless nephew. Good riddance to bad rubbish, I say."

"She shouldn't have asked him to come here," Emily said.

Hannah, obviously eager to avoid more questions about Dolly, did something she would not have done in a more cautious moment. She pulled a crumpled telegram from her pocket.

"Yes, that was Patterson's story, that she asked him, but it isn't true. I found this in the pocket of her dress."

"Her dress!" said Emily in surprise, and Hannah's eyes flicked away, not wanting to acknowledge that she had stooped to search a servant's room.

However, there was the telegram. *Am coming to manage things myself. You are too careful, dear aunt.*

"What things?" Emily asked. (Pushing Lucie out of her window?)

But the secrecy had come over Hannah's face again. She had already said too much.

"That's Patterson's and Raymond's affair. I imagine he didn't want to wait any longer for the balance of her savings. He has a Career. The selfish little monster!"

"And you don't believe a word of that, Cousin Hannah!" Emily said bleakly.

"Then can you, with your young eyes, find a better explanation? I advise you to stop asking questions." Hannah's voice was short, harsh, and unfriendly. "It's bad manners and none of the answers can do you any good. In any case, who is ever innocent?"

Lucie moved on the pillow. Her forehead was knitted in painful concentration.

"If only I could remember . . ."

"Remember what?" her mother said unsympathetically.

"A sound at the window last night. I *can't* remember . . ."

CHAPTER FOURTEEN

THE only place in which Emily could grow even remotely calm was Patrick's studio. She went there after she had left Lucie's room. She hadn't been able to stay another moment listening to Lucie's voice and wondering and suspecting about the shadow of some much older tragedy in Hannah's face.

She herself wasn't innocent, as Hannah knew. She had fallen in love with Patrick. She also knew that she could love Juana, the strange ethereal disturbed little girl who had only to be helped out of her neurosis.

But she had not fallen into this state deliberately. It had been a natural and unpreventable happening. She would go away, if she must. If she really must. She supposed she would even recover, as she had recovered from the abrupt end to her career. It would break her heart to leave Patrick and Juana, but better that than to be corrupted by the strange creeping disease that seemed to infest this lovely old Spanish house. An unidentified disease that destroyed people, making them cold, crafty, unable to love. A disease that had begun when two young girls had met there, lovely impulsive warm-hearted Dolly and her plain righteous cousin Hannah. . . .

It was only half past ten. The day already seemed to stretch into weeks. Emily walked up and down Patrick's studio, making herself study the glowing canvases, trying to project herself back into the mood that had made the day in Toledo so enchanting. Sunshine, the taste of wine, Patrick's eyes in an unguarded moment of happiness.

But the ugly present was too compelling. There were no

innocents here, as Hannah had said. Raymond, meaning only to be occupied with his sordid intention of extracting money from old women, had stumbled on some much bigger secret and run away. Surely that was the reason for his flight.

And wouldn't she do well to do the same?

No, she thought fiercely. She would stay until it was an impossibility. She was as illogical as all people in love, and convinced that she could bring nothing but good to those she loved. When that was no longer possible it would be time to go.

She would not be like Dolly, a deluded ghost who thought another woman's husband and baby her own. Poor Dolly who had had so much and finally had been reduced to begging crumbs from Hannah's table. . . .

It couldn't happen again! Hannah had cried, in fear and horror.

It would be dreadful, Emily thought, if she were so reduced in pride as to beg from Lucie. But it would be a state for pity, not that dry-eyed horror of Hannah's, as if she were looking on a long-hidden skeleton.

So that if the life story of the Bowman girls was repeating itself, could it have been Hannah who had been the thief? Hannah who had stolen Dolly's husband and child.

That would account for Hannah's extreme agitation, Emily thought feverishly.

But it did seem a highly improbable explanation. How could plain Hannah have accomplished such a thing? What terrible hold could she have had over Dolly?

Why didn't Patrick come back? He knew something. He had made a discovery on that trip to Toledo. He should have told her what it was.

But he had wanted to be sure first. There were records to be looked up to prove his suspicions. He had had to wait, and in the meantime Lucie had nearly died.

The house in the Calle de Fatima, Raymond's sudden departure, Hannah crying out in her loud strong voice when Emily had said that Lucie must be mad. . . .

"Emily!"

Patrick was calling to her. She couldn't help the elation that rushed through her at the sound of his voice. What a crazy state she was in, torn between agony and this kind of glory all the time. Momentarily she forgot Hannah, Dolly, all the ghosts.

"I'm here, waiting for you."

He ran up the steps. "Look out of the window."

The window was framed with the brilliant unreal blue of morning glory. As if it were a painting, a Spanish old master, perhaps, she saw the portly figure of Fabrice with an old woman on his arm entering the arched doorway into the courtyard. The two stood still a moment, Fabrice's head bent to his companion as if she were reluctant and he urging her. They were both in black. Silhouetted against the white stone, the stillness and the old woman's ashen cloud of hair made them even more like a painting. Something that had happened long ago . . .

Emily felt Patrick beside her.

"Who is it?" she whispered, and then didn't need to be told. "You found her in the house in the Calle de Fatima!"

"Fabrice did. He was there when I arrived."

"He had known all the time?"

"Yes."

Emily watched the two figures move forward again, Fabrice leading the old woman very gently, as if he expected the least sound to startle her.

"She's nervous and bewildered," said Patrick. "Which is natural since she hasn't been in the habit of paying visits for a very long time."

"It's La Loca," Emily said, almost reflectively.

"She's perfectly quiet, Pilar says. Don't be afraid."

Emily felt herself trembling with emotion. "I'm not afraid. But why is she here?"

"Because we discovered that the house in the Calle de Fatima belonged to our old friend, Don Jaime of Toledo."

"Do you mean that's his wife. It's true he shut her up!"

"She isn't his wife. But Fabrice will tell you."

This was the mysterious thing everyone had been afraid of, that one day the invisible menacing old woman from the house in the Calle de Fatima would be in their midst. Why?

Before she heard the answer to those things Emily had a more urgent thought.

"Juana mustn't see her! I must go to her."

"Juana will have to see her eventually," Patrick said. "And lay her own small private ghost. But you're right, it mustn't be sprung on her. There's a lot I have to tell you, Emily."

"Later," said Emily. "Let's find Juana first."

They hurried down the steps and towards the courtyard.

But they were not hurrying as much as Patterson. She came in just after them, her brown coat flapping, her hat slightly crooked. She looked as if she had been running in the hot morning sun. Her face was purpled, her eyes distended.

"Is it true?" she gasped, with what breath she had left. "Has she been brought here? Pilar said Mr. Fabrice had come for her."

"Pilar spoke the truth," Patrick answered.

"Oh, dear heaven, it will kill the mistress!"

Patterson made to go, but Emily caught her arm, holding her back.

"Why do you say that?"

A lifetime of subservient manners failed Patterson in that moment.

"Because it's Miss Dolly, you fool!"

Strangely, now that the extraordinary explanation had come, Emily had a feeling that she had always known it subconsciously. For Dolly had been as much a part of the *Casa de Flor* as if she had been living in it.

"Patrick, how long have you known this?"

"Only since we were in Madrid and your interest in Dolly's grave led me to the discovery that there was no record of any Dolly Bowman having died. Certainly she had been admitted to the English hospital. Both she and Hannah. The records said that both had been discharged, recovered. So Hannah had brought Dolly back to Granada. Where was she? If she was still alive there was only one place and one person she could be. La Loca living in the house in the Calle de Fatima, and a legend to which no one paid any attention until Juana was old enough to hear it."

"Before Miss Juana there was no trouble," Patterson said harshly. "Nobody bothered. Even then, if you hadn't come," she looked at Emily accusingly, "nothing would have been stirred up. But since you've been here there's been stirring, stirring, stirring."

Patterson's voice was full of bitter resentment, but telling the truth seemed to have eased her panic. She stood there still breathing heavily, an old overweight woman who had hurried too much in the hot Spanish sun.

"I wouldn't go in yet," Patrick said. "Let Fabrice get her composed first."

"Will she recognize—anybody?"

"You mean Hannah? I don't know. We'll see presently."

Unexpectedly Patterson's lip trembled. She had held in the truth too long. Now it was going to pour out of her.

"I always loved Miss Dolly. I visited her every week. Pilar will tell you. I never neglected her. Not that she knew me any more."

"When did this all begin?" Emily asked.

"I don't really know. I was only a servant. I just saw that Miss Hannah soon began bossing everything, and Don Jaime disappeared, and Miss Dolly broke her sweet heart and lost her reason."

"So you thought it would be ironic justice if Hannah lost hers." Patrick looked at Patterson without pity.

"No, no, I never meant that."

"But you meant other things," Patrick said grimly. "You and your cowardly nephew."

"If the mistress could have her here—" Patterson darted a look of enmity at Emily, and Patrick said:

"I know. Your tyranny had been a comparatively petty one until then. Only lining your nest very comfortably. But Master Raymond had bigger ideas."

"How was I to know?" Patterson moaned.

"What is this about?" Emily asked.

"Patterson has been blackmailing Hannah for a long time, with the threat of telling about Dolly. She was paying for her nephew's education and gathering capital for him, she said. But then Raymond got too greedy. He had guessed what was going on and thought it was going on too slowly. He would come and hasten the process. It was amusing making Hannah sell her French clock and the Meissen dinner service. But not so amusing when someone began to realize what might be going on. My wife," said Patrick, looking at Patterson stonily.

Patterson's face had lost its ruddy color. She no longer looked as if she had been too long in the sun. She looked cold and pinched.

"I did nothing, Mr. Patrick, I swear it."

"But you were worried that Lucie might have heard a conversation between you and Raymond. Weren't you? Because you and that unprepossessing young man parted rather hastily as Lucie came out of her room. Raymond said, 'The door was open!' as if he had got a nasty shock. As it happened, it was I who heard him, not Lucie. I admit I heard nothing else, if that gives you any satisfaction. I forgot the whole thing until after Lucie's accident. Then I put two and two together and realized that you weren't taking any risks. You had arranged for Raymond to call to Lucie from the maze after you knew she had taken sleeping pills. Am I right?"

"Raymond doesn't tell me everything he does." Patterson's eyes, even though terrified, were still spiteful. "He's not the boy I thought he was. If he called to Miss Lucie I didn't know."

"But, strangely enough, you knew the exact moment to go into her room. When she was leaning over the balcony."

Patterson sat down heavily on the wooden seat in the shade of the orange tree.

"I didn't touch her, sir! You can never prove I did. It was the pills that made her dizzy. She lost her balance and fell."

Patrick's eyes bored into hers.

"Can you live with that, Patterson?"

A touch of brazenness came back to Patterson.

"Yes, sir, I can. What's it compared to the mistress's behaviour all these years? If I'm wicked I've caught it from her. And she's gone scotfree."

"Has she?" said Patrick. His voice was heavy and sad. "We'll see."

Hannah was coming down the stairs very slowly. When she saw Emily and Patrick she paused and said, "Fabrice tells me there is someone important to see me. I had to dress without Patterson. So annoying. Who is this exceptional visitor?"

In spite of having to dress without Patterson's help, Hannah had put on her mantilla of smoky grey lace, and her long jade ear-rings. Her face beneath this finery was sunken and old, but interest in the unknown guest had roused her to her old alertness. Her topaz eyes gleamed. She was expecting the caller to be a wealthy customer who would perhaps buy the rejected tapestries, or some other treasure. Could she so easily forget her private troubles? Emily marvelled; then remembered that she had been living with them for a very long time. Lovely Dolly had endured her lonely life for half a lifetime.

Emily knew she should be repelled by Hannah. But in this moment, as she overcame her considerable infirmity and came downstairs unaided, her eyes alight for battle, she was a magnetic old creature whom it was impossible not to admire.

She should have sat for Goya. He would have interpreted her kindness and her ability to love as well as her formidable sins.

In any case, who was to judge until the whole story was heard?

"Is Patterson back yet?" Hannah asked, her voice carefully non-committal. "Has she accomplished her errand?"

"She's back," Patrick said. "She seems a little overcome by the heat."

"The heat! Patterson!" Hannah's eyes flashed. She was disturbed, but this was not the moment to worry about Patterson and her mysterious errand. (Had it been to give the old dragon Pilar more money to keep Dolly better hidden?)

"Tell her to stay in her room and rest until I need her. Now. Who is Fabrice surprising me with?"

She continued her slow, stately progress and exclaimed in irritation when Patrick walked at her side.

"Don't do that. I don't want a stranger to think me a cripple."

"You're magnificent, Mamita. But even you are going to have to give in some time."

Emily wondered if Hannah heard the extreme tenderness and sad affection in Patrick's voice. She hoped she did, for her shock a moment later, as she pushed open the door of the big cool living-room, was surely near to being fatal. Automatically she flung out her arm to Patrick for support. Anchored there she stood as still as stone.

At last she whispered in a hoarse voice, "Who has played this trick on me? Patterson? That old devil! I'll kill her!"

"Not Patterson, Mama," said Fabrice. "I did it. I thought a change of scenery a good idea for my mother."

There followed a silence that Emily thought would never end. And the whole picture was fitting into place before Fabrice went on, "She is my mother, isn't she? I realised that when Emily told me about that portrait in the *Palacio del Sol.* It explained a lot that has bothered me. Don Jaime was my father, wasn't he? And this is my mother."

"Fabrice! How dared you—" Hannah's stick tapped agitatedly. "She was well looked after. I saw to that."

"Perhaps. But she belongs here. This is her house. So I've brought her home."

The exquisite Dolly, the fabulous Dolly, mad, adorable Dolly as her many admirers had called her, was a white-haired old woman with a porcelain skin and thistledown hair. She sat beside Fabrice on the couch, one hand trustingly in his. She was like a doll. Her faded flower-like blue eyes were quite empty.

"The house isn't hers," Hannah said harshly. "It's mine. She gave it to me." Hannah was summoning her tenacious strength to meet this last challenge. "Very well, Fabrice, since you insist on knowing. Dolly gave me the house in return for assuming your parentage. That's why I married Ferdie. He agreed to be your father. You were born quite respectably as the child of Hannah and Ferdinand Romero. No one knows the truth but her," she indicated Dolly, "and she's forgotten it. And," Hannah's face darkened, "Patterson. I trusted Patterson. But for some reason she grew to hate me."

"And who else is hating me?" She flung her head round. "Don't be afraid to admit it. I'm used to it. Even my husband only married me for the money we knew we could get from Dolly. And this house. The *Casa de Flor*. I thought it was a palace. Me, straight from being a servant, living in other people's houses." Her face twisted. "It hasn't been a palace although I tried to make it like one. And Ferdie and I were happy enough, eventually. We had Lucie a long time after we thought we were never going to have children." Her voice was harsh, driven. "I told Lucie never to fall in love. That was the way to be unhappy. I'm sorry, Patrick. But it's the truth."

"We don't hate you, Mamita," said Patrick. "But you must tell us everything."

"Yes, Cousin Hannah," Emily urged.

Hannah groped for a chair and sat down.

"I'd speak to her but she wouldn't know me," she said, staring hypnotically at the small creature beside Fabrice.

"Go on, Mamita," said Patrick.

"What else is there to tell? I came to Spain to save Dolly from a disastrous marriage and found her expecting the child of Don Jaime. She said the nightingales had bewitched her. Faugh! I never had any patience with her romantics."

"And so they didn't marry," Patrick prodded. "Why?"

"Because a Spanish nobleman doesn't make a shotgun marriage," Hannah snapped. "Don Jaime disappeared and Dolly, who had never been very stable mentally—you could tell that by the way she rushed around flirting and falling in love indiscriminately—lost her reason having the child. Perhaps you've guessed already that she didn't have typhus, she had premature labour pains on that ghastly journey to Madrid. It was I who was developing typhus. If you can imagine that journey you might pity me. Dolly went out of her mind, and even I began to have delusions that I really was having that baby. You, Fabrice. You were a fine big baby and nearly killed your mother."

"Didn't I?" said Fabrice sadly.

"But before this terrible journey you had managed to extract her fortune from Dolly," went on Patrick's implacable voice.

"It was a bargain. I told you," Hannah said irritably. "Ferdie and I were to give the baby a name. And Dolly was to share our home, of course, and keep her respectability. Respectability meant everything in those days. But she had to be shut up when she lost her mind. That was imperative."

"So you prevailed on Don Jaime to give her a house and an income."

"Didn't he owe it to her? And someone had to pay Pablo and Pilar. Goodness knows, they've feathered their nests." Hannah was fast regaining her confidence. "Anyway, I always was a good business woman."

"Then why, Hannah," that was still Patrick, "did you insist on Emily seeing Don Jaime's home? The *Palacio del Sol*. Why were you so pleased when she said she had no desire to live in a castle? Were you hoping Dolly's answer would have been the same? Were you suffering remorse, by any chance?"

"Who doesn't?" said Hannah, looking at Patrick suspiciously.

"Who doesn't, indeed. But surely this was specific remorse. As if you had once ruined Dolly's chances of living in a castle."

"I told you. Dolly ruined her own chances. Who wanted a baby born at the altar? Not Don Jaime. He was proud. You don't know pride until you meet a Spanish grandee."

"And yet he never married," Patrick speculated. "He must have loved Dolly very much. Almost enough not to mind about that premature baby. If, indeed, he knew about it."

Hannah turned on him, her eyes flaring. "What are you hinting at?"

"I'm not hinting. I'm only wondering how Patterson has been able to blackmail you so successfully for so long."

"She's had thousands," said Fabrice heavily. "Since the business has gone down I've been at my wit's end. And then Mama's been making those expensive mistakes in her buying.

But I had to stand by her. I didn't know the whole truth. I only thought it important to avoid a scandal. I imagined Mama had cheated Dolly out of her fortune. Nothing more. If she was out of her senses she had to be kept under supervision, of course."

"And who sent her that way?" Emily had to move aside as Patterson came bursting into the room. "I've stood at the door and heard every word that's been said. And you haven't heard the whole truth by a long chalk. Oh, madam!" She pointed a quivering finger at Hannah. "You're whitewashing yourself as usual. You forget to say that you sent Don Jaime away because you told him Dolly had the seeds of madness in her. That was why her family had sent her to Spain. You said her mother had been mad, and her aunt. Such a lie! And all because you couldn't bear her to marry before you, and make such a brilliant marriage. All because you and that Spanish peasant wanted to get your hands on her money. And there was Miss Dolly as sane as you or me. Until grief, and you, working on her night and day, drove her out of her mind. 'Dolly, you must be mad,' I've heard you saying over and over. 'Your family always said you were unstable,' you used to say. 'From a little girl you did odd things. You should see the look in your eyes. It frightens me. No wonder it frightened your lover.' Oh, I've heard you, madam. And I've thought, some day, some day I'll pay Miss Dolly back for what she's suffered. I'll have her revenge for her."

"If listening at doors—aids your objective," Hannah said, with difficulty, "you promise to be—most successful."

But Patterson wasn't listening. She had gone across the room and fallen on her knees in front of the woman on the couch.

"I've always loved you, Miss Dolly. Truly I have. Welcome home."

It was no use attempting to rouse the quiet little creature with the thistledown hair. Her blue eyes simply looked placidly into the distance.

Until Juana came in.

She had run away from Maria who had been told to look after her. "Come back, you are not permitted in there," Maria called agitatedly. But Juana wanted to show Fabrice that her new doll's dress had been washed and mended and now she liked the doll again. She came flying in, paying no heed to Maria.

Immediately she saw Dolly she stood stockstill, her face whitening.

"La Loca!" she whispered.

Dolly saw the doll and stretched out her hands for it. Perhaps some memory of her lost baby stirred. For a moment her face was animated with an eerie loveliness.

Then Juana screamed.

"Mummy! Mummy! It's La Loca! She wants my doll again. Mummy!"

"Juana, stop!" Patrick cried, but the child had evaded him and rushed out of the room, giving her piercing shrieks.

Immediately, Emily knew the inevitable result. Hearing Juana, Lucie would get out of bed and come hastening to find her. Although Emily was the first to hurry out of the room to go to her, it was too late. Already Lucie was at the top of the stairs.

She stood there in her thin nightgown, swaying a little from dizziness, her dark hair falling over her shoulders. As Juana continued to shriek in her uncontrollable hysteria, Lucie held out her arms and began to run down the stairs towards her daughter.

"Juana, honey!" Emily heard her say. "It's all right. I'm coming." And that was the exact moment when her unsteady feet tripped and she fell headlong. She tumbled all the way down the stairs, and at last lay still, her head twisted at an unnatural angle.

Patterson had extracted her final payment much more terribly than she had meant to. Dolly was revenged at last.

Later, the innocent and unconscious cause of Lucie's death —for there was no reviving her from her second fall—sat on Hannah's chair, the one that had once belonged to a cardinal, and smiled gently and said that she thought she could hear a canary singing.

"Patterson, where did you put the canary?"

Patterson, her face still blotched with tears, said, "Oh, Miss Dolly, you mean the one we brought from England? It—" She recollected herself and lied smoothly, "It's on the balcony."

She turned to Emily, nothing more now than an old sad tired empty woman, and said, "She's always been like that, quite happy listening to the birds and making herself new dresses. Or what she thinks are dresses. The yards of lace and ribbon I've taken her. And roses. She'd be happy for days with an artificial rose."

"Does Hannah know this?" Emily asked.

Patterson's voice went sullen. "I don't know. If she did she preferred not to see. I did it myself. Out of my ill-gotten gains," she added with -acid irony. "I didn't spend them all on Raymond. And I spent nothing on myself."

"But didn't you see what Hannah was doing at the beginning? Couldn't you have stopped her?"

"I believed her," Patterson said bitterly. "I didn't trust foreigners myself in those days. So I believed what Miss Hannah said about Don Jaime. Miss Dolly was—well, scatter-brained, you know, and I thought myself she was behaving a bit wild over that Spaniard. I was quite pleased to see him go. But I didn't know then about the baby or the means Miss Hannah had used. I couldn't repair all that. It was done. So I just did little things to make my poor Miss Dolly happy over all these years. Oh, I know I've been wicked. But not as wicked as her." She cast a malevolent glance upwards in the direction of Hannah's bedroom where Hannah was sleeping after heavy sedation by the doctor. "She's got her deserts."

"Lucie didn't deserve what she got," Emily said.

"It was fate," said Patterson sombrely. She looked critically at Emily's white face. "Now don't you go breaking down, miss. The child needs you."

"Do you think so, Patterson?" Emily's eyes filled with tears. She was not without guilt either. She had caused poor tragic Lucie pain because she had, unpreventably, acquired the love of both her husband and child. But now Lucie was gone, through no fault of Emily's or Patrick's, and it was senseless to refuse happiness.

"I should never say it, miss, but Miss Lucie was going to destroy even more than her mother did. It was in her nature. You—I didn't want you here and I saw no reason to like you—but I've got sense enough to see that you wouldn't destroy. You're what Miss Dolly could have been." Patterson blinked rapidly and said roughly, "Then you'd better go and see to the child. She'll be waking up any time. She shouldn't be alone after that shock this morning."

"She doesn't know her mother's dead. She thinks she's been taken to the hospital. But you're right, Patterson. She shouldn't be alone. As soon as she's awake I'll bring her down here."

"Here! And have her throw another fit. You know she'll scream her head off at the sight of—" Patterson indicated Dolly sitting serenely in the splendid chair.

"They'll make friends," said Emily. "They're both children."

When Juana at last stirred awake (the doctor had given her also a small sedative to tide her over the immediate shock of her mother's accident) her eyes immediately flew to Emily.

"Mummy?" she asked in a tentative voice.

"She's not here, darling," Emily said steadily. "Daddy's taken her away to get better. Daddy will be back. Soon," she added, wishing Patrick were here at this moment to begin recovering from his own shock and misery.

"She fell downstairs. I saw her. I saw her tumbling and falling."

"Come here," said Emily, holding out her arms. "Sit on my lap for a little while."

Juana obeyed. She felt as light as a leaf, as a shadow. Her bird bones pressed into Emily's flesh. But her eyes were quietening.

Presently Emily said, "I want you to put on your prettiest dress because we have a visitor."

Juana's head shot up.

"Who? Not—not—"

"Your Great-aunt Dolly, darling. Oh, and do you know, we've quite forgotten that poor little handkerchief doll we left in the piano. Come, choose your dress and I'll brush your hair. Then we'll go and rescue the doll."

"You said she had to live in the piano."

"Well—sometimes she may like a little social life."

"What's social life?" Juana asked, wary but interested.

"It's people talking politely together, as you're going to talk to your Great-aunt Dolly in a little while."

At the door Juana hung back, her face taut.

"It is her!" she hissed. "It is La Loca."

Emily held her hand firmly.

"How blind you are! Can't you see it's your Great-aunt Dolly? Look, she's smiling at you."

"It's—but it *is* La Loca, Emily!" Juana's whisper was panic-stricken. "She'll take this doll, too!"

"You're going to give it to her," said Emily calmly. "It will please her."

Juana pulled back frantically. But she didn't scream. Then, after that initial moment of panic, the miracle happened. She stiffened her small body and walked rapidly across to Dolly, thrusting the cloth doll into her hands. Immediately, she flew back to Emily, trembling but triumphant.

"I did it! I was scared, but I gave it to her!"

Emily's eyes were wet.

"Yes, you did. And look, she likes it."

Juana took a swift backwards glance at the old lady who was examing the doll with great interest. She began to giggle. "She's too old for dolls, really. But if she likes them that much, I suppose I could show her my new one."

"I suppose you could, honey. Run and get it."

When Patrick came in Juana was sitting on the floor at Dolly's feet earnestly demonstrating how a doll should be dressed.

"Oh, no, Great-aunt Dolly, the petticoats come first. *Before* the dress. Excuse me, but you are a little stupid. Watch me, I'll show you."

"What miracle have you worked now?" Patrick asked Emily.

"Not a miracle. Only commonsense. They're both children." She added, looking at his gaunt face, "Juana's lucky. Her ghost was easy to lay."

"Hannah?"

"She's still sleeping."

"Good. Fabrice will be back soon. We've—made all the arrangements. But the household will have to be reorganized."

"Don't worry about it now." Emily longed to take the tiredness and shock out of his face. "Dolly thinks there's a canary singing on the balcony."

"She's lucky, too. She can take her canaries with her."

The emptiness of Patrick's voice made Emily seize him with both arms.

"Patrick, let's get away from here. As soon as we can. With Juana. You never belonged here, and I don't intend to. We've been caught in a tragedy that's none of our business. It's fifty years old. They must work it out for themselves. Patrick!" She searched his face. "This is true! I'll make you believe it."

At last there was the flicker of a smile in his eyes.

"I don't doubt you. If you can make Juana forget her

nightmares so quickly, heaven only knows what you can do with me. I'm not such unresponsive material as my daughter. But gently, my darling. Let the dust settle."

CHAPTER FIFTEEN

"I SHALL sell everything in the house," Fabrice was saying with the firmness he had acquired in the last few days.

"Everything!" Hannah exclaimed. "But I've spent a lifetime gathering these things."

"For a rainy day," Fabrice said. "It rains even in Spain. The house will have to go, too."

"Not the *Casa de Flor!*"

"I'll find you a smaller place. I shall live over the shop myself."

"And keep nothing but your clocks and child's toys." Hannah could still be scathing.

"As I've always wanted to."

Hannah reflected. "So there'll be just the three of us."

"That's right. You and Dolly and Patterson. As you were in the beginning. It's quite a neat ending."

"If you like neat endings," Hannah said with her old asperity. She added with uncharacteristic quietness, "It is an ending. No one can deny that."

Then she held out her hand to Emily.

"Do you forgive a wicked foolish old woman? I had this feeling that I could make amends to Dolly by giving you a chance of happiness. You were so like her. Patterson said I was in my dotage. Or mad."

Emily met her entreating gaze.

"Not mad, Cousin Hannah."

"I never realised how much I loved Dolly until I had done that terrible thing to her. That couldn't be undone. So I loved you instead." She held Emily's hand against her cheek. "What will you do now?"

"Patrick has his exhibition in Madrid. I'm helping him. He wants me to. After that—" (Patrick had said nothing about what would happen after that, but it was there in his eyes, the unabashed unconcealable love.) "We're taking Juana, you know," she said.

Hannah inclined her head.

"She's going to be all right, Cousin Hannah. I hate to say this to you, but her mother's love weighed too heavily on her. She was too young, too little."

"I know. So all isn't lost." Hannah spoke quite briskly. "You must go away and forget us, Emily. The Bowman girls. Dolly the pretty, Hannah the plain. We're past history. Patterson will take good care of us. We may even eventually live on her savings." Hannah gave her sudden raucous chuckle. She hadn't lost her spirit. She would still extract what ironic humour she could from the situation. She might even begin to enjoy herself again.

"But for you, Emily, you must do what you came to do. Go sight-seeing, stay in the villages, learn to speak the language, listen to the church bells, fall in love with the sun."

"I will," said Emily. "I have."

"Have you kept that old marriage chest? It's not to be sold, tell Fabrice."

"He knows, Cousin Hannah."

"So all isn't lost," said Hannah again, very quietly. For the first time since Emily had known her there was a glimmer of peace in her face.

FAWCETT CREST BOOKS

ON TOP WITH
THE BIG BESTSELLERS

WHO DO YOU THINK YOU ARE, CHARLIE BROWN?
by Charles M. Schulz   (D1089)   50¢

THAT QUAIL, ROBERT   by Margaret A. Stanger   (R1090)   60¢

PHYLLIS DILLER'S HOUSEKEEPING HINTS
by Phyllis Diller   (R1082)   60¢

THE LAST ONE LEFT   by John D. MacDonald   (T1085)   75¢

AFTER THE ACT   by Winston Graham   (R1087)   60¢

CASTLE UGLY   by Mary Ellin Barrett   (T1076)   75¢

THE COUNTRY TEAM   by Robin Moore   (M1069)   95¢

APPENDIX TO THE I HATE TO COOK BOOK
by Peg Bracken   (D1063)   50¢

NO ONE HEARS BUT HIM   by Taylor Caldwell   (T1054)   75¢

GILES GOAT-BOY   by John Barth   (P1052) $1.25

SATURDAY THE RABBI WENT HUNGRY
by Harry Kemelman   (R1036)   60¢

COLUMBELLA   by Phyllis A. Whitney   (T1037)   75¢

ECSTASY AND ME   by Hedy Lamarr   (T1035)   75¢

MENFREYA IN THE MORNING   by Victoria Holt   (T1020)   75¢

I, THE KING   by Frances Parkinson Keyes   (T1021)   75¢

THE DOUBLE IMAGE   by Helen MacInnes   (T1013)   75¢

A THOUSAND DAYS   by Arthur Schlesinger, Jr.   (A1000) $1.65

THE SOURCE   by James A. Michener   (A995) $1.65

THE HONEY BADGER   by Robert Ruark   (M962)   95¢

THE RABBI   by Noah Gordon   (M954)   95¢

THE I HATE TO HOUSEKEEP BOOK
by Peg Bracken   (D830)   50¢

THE I HATE TO COOK BOOK   by Peg Bracken   (D777)   50¢

A Fawcett ⟡ *Crest Reprint*

Wherever Paperbacks Are Sold

"MARY STEWART IS ONE OF THE MOST EXCITING DISCOVERIES OF RECENT YEARS. . . . DON'T MISS HER EVER."
—*Boston Globe*

AIRS ABOVE THE GROUND   T969   75¢

"A tale of breathless excitement against a background of breathless scenic beauty."
—*Cleveland Plain Dealer*

NINE COACHES WAITING   R774   60¢

"A wonderful hue-and-cry story . . . a Mona Lisa tale that beckons you on while suspense builds up."
—*Boston Herald*

MY BROTHER MICHAEL   T1106   75¢

". . . all the suspense and danger anybody could demand . . ."
—*New York Herald Tribune*

MADAM, WILL YOU TALK?   R862   60¢

"Unusually skillful . . . headlong urgency of action."
—*Anthony Boucher*
The New York Times

THUNDER ON THE RIGHT   R894   60¢

"A highly charged romantic thriller."
—*New York Herald Tribune*

THE IVY TREE   T823   75¢

"Perils await every turning page."
—*Washington Post*

THE MOON-SPINNERS   T1110   75¢

"Here is magical writing . . . a story of breathless suspense . . . seasoned with spirit and humor."
—*Los Angeles Times*

WILDFIRE AT MIDNIGHT   R893   60¢

"Terror in the Hitchcock manner . . . a novel that terrifies as it entertains."
—*Columbus Dispatch*

A Fawcett Crest Reprint

Wherever Paperbacks Are Sold